# The Miracles of Elisha

**Christian fiction, Volume 6**

Gregory Allen Parker

Published by Graywolf Press, 2024.

This is a work of fiction. Similarities to real people, places, or events are entirely coincidental.

THE MIRACLES OF ELISHA

**First edition. August 7, 2024.**

Copyright © 2024 Gregory Allen Parker.

ISBN: 979-8227090393

Written by Gregory Allen Parker.

# Table of Contents

To all who seek the wonders of faith,

This book is dedicated to the unsung heroes of faith who, like Elisha, follow the call of the divine with unwavering trust and commitment. To those who face life's challenges with courage and rely on God's miracles, may you find inspiration and strength in these pages.

To my family and friends, whose love and support have been my foundation, thank you for being my constant source of encouragement and belief.

And to the countless readers who embark on this journey, may the stories of Elisha's miracles renew your hope and deepen your faith in the boundless power of God's grace.

# Chapter 1: The Calling of Elisha

## Introduction to Elisha as a Young Man

In the fertile land of Abel-Meholah, a young man named Elisha, the son of Shaphat, lived a life deeply rooted in the soil of his inheritance. The valley of Abel-Meholah, nestled between rolling hills and the Jordan River, was a place of prosperity and hard work, where the people toiled from dawn until dusk. Here, the sun blazed down upon golden fields of grain, and the air was filled with the sounds of labor and life. The land was generous to those who were diligent, and Elisha was among the most industrious of all.

Elisha was known for his strength and integrity. His hands were calloused from years of working the fields, and his back bore the muscle of a man accustomed to hard labor. Despite the physical demands of his work, Elisha's spirit was gentle, and he possessed a wisdom beyond his years. He was a man of deep thought and quiet contemplation, often found meditating on the words of the prophets and the laws of Moses.

Raised in a devout family, Elisha's upbringing was steeped in the traditions and faith of Israel. His father, Shaphat, was a respected landowner, and his household was one of piety and reverence for the God of Abraham, Isaac, and Jacob. From a young age, Elisha had been taught to honor the Sabbath, observe the festivals, and offer sacrifices according to the Law. The stories of the patriarchs and the miracles of God were as familiar to him as the seasons of planting and harvest.

Despite the wealth and comfort of his family, Elisha remained humble. He often joined the servants in their tasks, driving the oxen and plowing the fields alongside them. He found joy in the simple, honest work of tilling the soil and reaping the harvest. The rhythm of the seasons and the cycle of growth and renewal mirrored his own spiritual journey, fostering a deep connection to the land and to his Creator.

# Elijah's Prophetic Call to Elisha

It was in this setting, amidst the daily routines of farm life, that a remarkable event occurred—an event that would alter the course of Elisha's life and shape the destiny of Israel. The great prophet Elijah, a man whose name was revered and whose deeds were legendary, had been commanded by God to seek out Elisha and anoint him as his successor.

Elijah was a towering figure in Israel's history. Known for his fierce devotion to God and his bold confrontations with the idolatrous kings of Israel, Elijah's life was a testament to the power of unwavering faith. He had called down fire from heaven, ended a three-year drought with a prayer, and challenged the prophets of Baal on Mount Carmel. His presence inspired awe and fear, and his words carried the weight of divine authority.

As Elijah made his way to Abel-Meholah, the air seemed charged with anticipation. The prophet's journey was not taken lightly; it was a divine mission, and the mantle he carried was not merely a garment but a symbol of his prophetic office and the power of God's Spirit upon him.

Elisha was in the fields, as he was most days, driving the twelfth pair of oxen. The scene was one of typical industriousness, with the sun high in the sky and the sounds of animals and men blending into the harmonious symphony of a working farm. The plow dug deep into the rich earth, turning over the soil in preparation for planting. Elisha's thoughts were likely on the task at hand, unaware that his life was about to change forever.

As Elijah approached, his heart was full of the words that God had spoken to him. He saw Elisha and knew that this young man was chosen by God to continue his work. With purposeful steps, Elijah walked up to Elisha and threw his cloak around him. This act was deeply symbolic, signifying the transfer of prophetic authority and the calling of Elisha into a divine mission.

## Elisha's Decision to Follow Elijah

The moment the cloak settled on Elisha's shoulders, he felt an overwhelming presence, a sense of destiny that transcended the ordinary. The weight of the cloak was more than just physical; it carried the weight of a divine calling.

Elisha understood immediately what this meant. The stories of old, the tales of Samuel and David, came alive in his mind. This was a call from God Himself.

Without hesitation, Elisha stopped his work. He left the plow standing in the field and ran after Elijah. "Let me kiss my father and mother goodbye," he said, "and then I will come with you." (1 Kings 19:20). Elijah's response was simple and profound: "Go back. What have I done to you?" (1 Kings 19:20). This was not a dismissal but a recognition of Elisha's need to settle his affairs and the magnitude of the decision he was making.

Elisha returned to his family, but not to linger in comfort or delay his calling. He took the yoke of oxen and slaughtered them. He burned the plowing equipment to cook the meat and gave it to the people, and they ate. Then he set out to follow Elijah and became his servant (1 Kings 19:21). This act was a powerful statement of commitment and sacrifice. Elisha was severing his ties to his past life, abandoning his earthly security to embrace the unknown journey ahead.

Elisha's decision was a profound demonstration of faith and obedience. He did not know what lay ahead, but he trusted in God's plan. The burning of the plow and the slaughter of the oxen symbolized a total and irreversible commitment to his new calling. It was a declaration that there was no turning back, no retreating to the familiar comforts of his former life.

From that day forward, Elisha followed Elijah, learning from him, serving him, and preparing to take up the mantle of prophecy. His journey would be one of great trials and miraculous deeds, but it began with a simple act of obedience and a profound leap of faith.

## Bible Verse: 1 Kings 19:19-21

"So Elijah went from there and found Elisha son of Shaphat. He was plowing with twelve yoke of oxen, and he himself was driving the twelfth pair. Elijah went up to him and threw his cloak around him. Elisha then left his oxen and ran after Elijah. 'Let me kiss my father and mother goodbye,' he said, 'and then I will come with you.' 'Go back,' Elijah replied. 'What have I done to you?' So Elisha left him and went back. He took his yoke of oxen and slaughtered them. He burned the plowing equipment to cook the meat and gave it to the people, and they ate. Then he set out to follow Elijah and became his servant."

# Reflections on the Calling of Elisha

The calling of Elisha is a powerful story of divine selection and human response. It is a narrative that speaks to the heart of faith, sacrifice, and the willingness to step into the unknown at God's command. Elisha's life before his calling was one of routine and hard work, but it was precisely in this ordinary context that God chose to intervene.

Elijah's approach to Elisha was marked by a quiet authority and a profound understanding of God's will. The simplicity of his action—throwing his cloak over Elisha—belies the profound significance of the moment. This was not just a transfer of a garment but a symbolic act of passing on a divine mission. Elisha's immediate recognition and acceptance of this calling highlight his spiritual readiness and deep faith.

Elisha's response, marked by the slaughter of the oxen and the burning of the plow, is a dramatic demonstration of his total commitment. It is a vivid illustration of the cost of discipleship. Elisha did not merely leave his old life behind; he made a definitive break with it, ensuring there was no possibility of return. This act of sacrifice echoes the calls to discipleship found throughout scripture, where following God often requires leaving behind the familiar and embracing a new, uncertain path.

This chapter in Elisha's life serves as an enduring lesson for all who seek to follow God's call. It reminds us that God often calls us out of our comfort zones, asking us to trust Him and take bold steps of faith. It teaches us that true discipleship involves sacrifice and a willingness to leave behind what is known and secure. Most importantly, it assures us that God's calling comes with His provision and guidance, just as Elisha would come to experience in his journey as a prophet.

# Elisha's Early Years and Preparation

Before the dramatic encounter with Elijah, Elisha's life in Abel-Meholah had been one of preparation, even if he had not realized it at the time. His upbringing in a faithful household, his work ethic, and his reflective nature were all shaping him for the role he would eventually play in God's plan. Each day spent in the fields, each prayer offered, and each scripture studied were steps on the path that led to his calling.

Elisha's relationship with his family was strong and supportive. Shaphat, his father, was a man of integrity and faith, instilling in Elisha the values that would guide him throughout his life. His mother, too, played a significant role in nurturing his spiritual growth. They taught him to honor God above all, to seek His will, and to trust in His provision. These foundational lessons were crucial as Elisha stepped into his new role.

The fields of Abel-Meholah were not just a place of labor but a place of communion with God. As Elisha worked, he often meditated on the words of the prophets, finding in them a source of strength and inspiration. The stories of Moses, Samuel, and Elijah resonated deeply with him, kindling a desire to serve God in whatever capacity he might be called.

Elisha's interactions with the servants and workers on his father's estate also prepared him for his prophetic ministry. He learned to lead with humility and to serve others with compassion. These qualities would become essential as he ministered to the people of Israel, offering them guidance, comfort, and the power of God's miracles.

## The Significance of Elijah's Cloak

The cloak that Elijah threw over Elisha was a symbol of prophetic authority and divine power. In ancient Israel, a prophet's mantle was more than just a piece of clothing; it was a representation of their office and the anointing of God's Spirit upon them. When Elijah placed his cloak on Elisha, it was a tangible sign that God had chosen Elisha to succeed him as His prophet.

This act of passing the mantle is rich with symbolic meaning. It signifies the continuity of God's work through successive generations. Just as Elijah had been called to confront the idolatry of Israel and lead the people back to God, so too would Elisha carry on this mission. The mantle represented the passing of responsibility and the empowerment to fulfill that responsibility.

Elisha's immediate response to the mantle shows his deep understanding of its significance. He did not hesitate or question the call; instead, he acted with decisive faith. This readiness to accept God's call is a testament to his spiritual maturity and his trust in God's plan.

## The Journey of Discipleship

Elisha's decision to follow Elijah was the beginning of a profound journey of discipleship. As he left behind his family and livelihood, he embarked on a path that would test his faith, refine his character, and reveal God's power in extraordinary ways. This journey was not just about following a prophet; it was about walking closely with God and being used by Him to accomplish His purposes.

The relationship between Elijah and Elisha was one of mentorship and growth. Elijah, as the seasoned prophet, provided guidance, wisdom, and a model of faithful service. Elisha, as the disciple, absorbed these lessons and prepared himself for the day when he would take up Elijah's mantle fully. Their time together was marked by significant events and miracles, each serving to strengthen Elisha's faith and readiness.

Elisha's commitment to follow Elijah, as seen in his immediate abandonment of his previous life, is a powerful example of what it means to be a true disciple. It involves a willingness to leave behind the old, embrace the new, and trust in God's provision and guidance. This radical commitment is a recurring theme in the Bible and a central aspect of the call to discipleship.

## The Impact of Elisha's Calling

The calling of Elisha had a profound impact on Israel's history. As he stepped into his role as a prophet, he became a vessel through which God performed many miracles and spoke His word to the people. Elisha's ministry was marked by acts of compassion, power, and divine intervention. He brought healing to the sick, provision to the needy, and guidance to those in distress.

Elisha's life and ministry serve as a powerful reminder of the importance of obedience to God's call. His willingness to leave behind his old life and follow God's leading resulted in a ministry that blessed countless lives and demonstrated the power of God's love and faithfulness. His story encourages believers to respond to God's call with faith and courage, trusting that He will provide and guide them in their journey.

The legacy of Elisha's calling is a testament to the transformative power of God's call and the impact of faithful obedience. It shows that when we respond to God's call, we become instruments of His grace and power, capable of influencing the world in ways beyond our imagination. Elisha's story continues to inspire and challenge believers to live lives of faith, commitment, and service.

## Conclusion

The calling of Elisha is a compelling narrative of divine intervention, human response, and the journey of discipleship. It highlights the importance of being ready to respond to God's call, the significance of mentorship and preparation, and the impact of faithful obedience. Elisha's life before and after his calling provides rich insights into the nature of God's work in the world and the role we are called to play in His plan.

Elisha's story is a timeless reminder that God often calls us out of our ordinary lives to do extraordinary things. It challenges us to be willing to leave behind what is comfortable and secure, to embrace the unknown with faith, and to trust in God's provision and guidance. As we reflect on Elisha's journey, we are encouraged to listen for God's call in our own lives and to respond with the same readiness and commitment that Elisha demonstrated.

Through Elisha's story, we see the power of God's call to transform lives and shape history. It is a story of faith, sacrifice, and divine purpose, inviting us to participate in the unfolding of God's plan for the world. As we follow Elisha's example, we too can experience the joy and fulfillment of living out our calling and witnessing the incredible ways God can use us for His glory.

# Chapter 2: Crossing the Jordan

## Elisha's Journey with Elijah

The journey of Elisha with Elijah was not merely a physical trek but a spiritual pilgrimage marked by profound lessons, divine encounters, and moments that tested and strengthened Elisha's resolve. From the time Elijah called Elisha by casting his cloak upon him, Elisha had committed himself to following the great prophet wherever he went, learning from him, and preparing to carry on his mission. This journey was to culminate in a momentous event that would both signify and solidify Elisha's prophetic calling.

Elisha, a man of humble beginnings, had grown into his role as Elijah's disciple with a mix of awe and devotion. The bond between the two prophets was one of deep mutual respect and spiritual camaraderie. Elijah, aware of his impending departure, was keen to impart as much wisdom and spiritual insight as possible to his young protégé. Elisha, in turn, absorbed everything with the fervor of one chosen by God for a great task.

Their journey took them through various cities and regions, each with its own significance and set of challenges. From Gilgal to Bethel, from Jericho to the Jordan River, each step was a step deeper into the understanding of God's work and His plans. The people they encountered, the miracles they witnessed, and the lessons they learned were all part of the divine curriculum designed to prepare Elisha for his future role.

## The Miraculous Parting of the Jordan River

As they approached the Jordan River, the air was thick with a sense of anticipation and divine presence. This river, which had played such a pivotal role in the history of Israel—from the crossing led by Joshua to the baptisms performed by John the Baptist—was now to witness another miraculous event. Elijah and Elisha stood at its banks, ready to cross over into a new chapter of their journey and, indeed, of Elisha's life.

Elijah took his cloak, the same cloak he had cast over Elisha to call him into prophetic service, and rolled it up. With a decisive gesture, he struck the water with it. Immediately, the waters of the Jordan divided to the right and to the left, creating a dry path for the two prophets to walk through. This miraculous parting was a powerful affirmation of Elijah's prophetic authority and the divine favor that rested upon him. It also served as a sign of the great things to come for Elisha.

As they crossed the Jordan on dry ground, Elisha's mind must have been racing with thoughts of the past and the future. He recalled the stories of how God had parted the Red Sea for Moses and the Jordan for Joshua. Now, he was part of a similar miracle, a direct witness to God's power and faithfulness. The significance of this moment was not lost on him. It was a confirmation of the path he had chosen and the divine mission he was about to inherit.

## Elisha's Commitment to Stay with Elijah Until the End

Throughout their journey, Elijah had tested Elisha's commitment multiple times. At Gilgal, Bethel, and Jericho, Elijah had told Elisha to stay behind while he moved on. Each time, Elisha had responded with unwavering resolve: "As surely as the Lord lives and as you live, I will not leave you." This steadfast determination was a testament to Elisha's loyalty and his understanding of the importance of his role.

The journey to the Jordan River was the final leg of this testing. Elisha knew that Elijah's departure was imminent, and he was determined to stay with his master until the very end. His commitment was not born out of mere duty but out of a profound sense of purpose and devotion to God's calling. Elisha understood that his place was by Elijah's side, learning, absorbing, and preparing for the moment when he would take up the mantle.

As they crossed the Jordan, Elijah turned to Elisha and asked, "Tell me, what can I do for you before I am taken from you?" (2 Kings 2:9). This question was both a challenge and an invitation, a final test of Elisha's vision and readiness for the prophetic office. Elisha's response was immediate and bold: "Let me inherit a double portion of your spirit." This request was not a plea for power but a humble recognition of the immense responsibility that lay ahead. Elisha sought the spiritual strength and wisdom to fulfill his calling faithfully and effectively.

Elijah's reply was both a blessing and a prophecy: "You have asked a difficult thing," Elijah said. "Yet if you see me when I am taken from you, it will be yours—otherwise, it will not" (2 Kings 2:10). This response underscored the need for spiritual vigilance and readiness. Elisha's request would be granted, but it required him to witness Elijah's departure, symbolizing his readiness to step into his master's shoes.

## Bible Verse: 2 Kings 2:8

"Elijah took his cloak, rolled it up and struck the water with it. The water divided to the right and to the left, and the two of them crossed over on dry ground."

## Reflections on Crossing the Jordan

The crossing of the Jordan River was more than a physical journey; it was a profound spiritual passage that marked the transition from one phase of Elisha's life to another. It symbolized the end of his apprenticeship under Elijah and the beginning of his own prophetic ministry. This event, steeped in biblical symbolism and divine power, was a defining moment for Elisha and for the people of Israel.

The act of striking the water with Elijah's cloak and the subsequent parting of the Jordan is reminiscent of the parting of the Red Sea by Moses. Both events signify God's intervention and provision, creating a path where there seemed to be none. For Elisha, this miracle was a powerful affirmation of God's presence and a sign that he was on the right path. It reinforced the lessons of faith, obedience, and divine power that he had learned from Elijah.

Elisha's unwavering commitment to stay with Elijah until the end reflects his deep understanding of the gravity of his calling. He recognized that his role was not just to witness miracles but to be a conduit of God's power and wisdom to the people. This commitment, tested and proven through the journey, was essential for the task ahead. Elisha's determination and faithfulness are qualities that all believers are called to emulate.

# The Significance of the Double Portion

Elisha's request for a double portion of Elijah's spirit is one of the most profound moments in this narrative. In ancient Israel, the firstborn son would receive a double portion of the inheritance, signifying his role as the leader of the family. By asking for a double portion, Elisha was expressing his desire to carry on Elijah's ministry with the same fervor and power, acknowledging the weight of the responsibility.

This request highlights Elisha's humility and his recognition of his need for divine empowerment. He understood that the task ahead was immense and that he could not accomplish it on his own strength. The double portion was not about personal glory but about being adequately equipped to fulfill God's purposes. It was a testament to Elisha's deep spiritual insight and his readiness to step into his prophetic role.

Elijah's response, pointing to the condition of witnessing his departure, underscores the importance of spiritual readiness and vigilance. The double portion was a gift that required Elisha to be fully present and aware, symbolizing his readiness to receive and steward God's power responsibly. This condition also served as a final affirmation of Elisha's commitment and faith.

# Elijah's Departure and Elisha's Ascension

As they continued their journey after crossing the Jordan, the moment of Elijah's departure drew near. They walked and talked, and Elijah imparted his final words of wisdom to Elisha. Suddenly, a chariot of fire and horses of fire appeared and separated the two of them, and Elijah went up to heaven in a whirlwind (2 Kings 2:11). Elisha saw this and cried out, "My father! My father! The chariots and horsemen of Israel!" (2 Kings 2:12).

Elisha's cry was one of deep emotion and recognition of the spiritual significance of the moment. Elijah's departure was not just the end of an era but the beginning of a new one. The chariots and horsemen of Israel symbolized God's power and protection, and Elijah's ascension was a powerful affirmation of his prophetic mission. Elisha's witness of this event was a confirmation of his own calling and the fulfillment of the condition for receiving the double portion.

Elisha picked up Elijah's cloak, which had fallen from him, and went back and stood on the bank of the Jordan. He took the cloak that had fallen from Elijah and struck the water with it. "Where now is the Lord, the God of Elijah?" he asked. When he struck the water, it divided to the right and to the left, and he crossed over (2 Kings 2:13-14). This act was a powerful declaration of Elisha's new role and the continuation of Elijah's ministry. It was a sign that God's power and presence were now with him.

## The Beginning of Elisha's Ministry

With the mantle of Elijah now firmly in his possession, Elisha began his prophetic ministry. The miracles and signs that followed were a testament to the double portion of Elijah's spirit that rested upon him. Elisha's first act was to repeat the miracle of the Jordan's parting, a clear indication that he was now God's chosen prophet for Israel.

Elisha's ministry was characterized by acts of compassion, power, and divine intervention. He healed the sick, provided for the needy, and performed miracles that revealed God's love and sovereignty. The journey with Elijah and the crossing of the Jordan had prepared him for these tasks, equipping him with the spiritual strength and wisdom needed to lead and guide the people.

The double portion of Elijah's spirit manifested in Elisha's life through his bold faith, his commitment to God's will, and his unwavering dedication to his prophetic mission. Elisha's ministry was a continuation of Elijah's, but it also had its unique aspects and challenges. Through it all, Elisha remained faithful to the calling he had received, demonstrating the power of God's Spirit working through him.

### Conclusion

The crossing of the Jordan marks a pivotal moment in the life of Elisha and the history of Israel. It is a story of divine calling, unwavering commitment, and the power of God's miracles. The journey with Elijah, the miraculous parting of the Jordan, and Elisha's bold request for a double portion of Elijah's spirit all highlight the profound spiritual lessons and the immense responsibility that come with God's call.

Elisha's story is a powerful reminder of the importance of faithfulness, humility, and readiness in responding to God's call. His journey with Elijah and the miraculous events he witnessed prepared him for a ministry that would impact countless lives and reveal God's power and love. As we reflect on Elisha's journey, we are encouraged to seek God's will with the same fervor, commitment, and faith that Elisha demonstrated.

Through the crossing of the Jordan, we see the continuity of God's work and the way He equips and empowers His servants to carry out His purposes. Elisha's life and ministry serve as a testament to the transformative power of God's call and the impact of faithful obedience. His story invites us to participate in the unfolding of God's plan, trusting in His provision and guidance as we step into the roles He has prepared for us.

# Chapter 3: Elijah's Ascension

## The Final Moments Between Elijah and Elisha

The bond between Elijah and Elisha had grown deeper with each passing day. From the moment Elijah had thrown his cloak over Elisha, marking his divine calling, their journey together had been one of profound spiritual significance. They traveled through the lands of Israel, encountering various communities, performing miracles, and delivering God's messages. Each experience further prepared Elisha for the moment when he would take over Elijah's mantle and continue the prophetic mission.

As the day of Elijah's departure drew near, there was an unspoken tension and anticipation. Elisha, fully aware of the impending transition, was determined to stay with Elijah until the very end. The two prophets moved from Gilgal to Bethel, and from Bethel to Jericho, each location imbued with its own spiritual importance and history. Elijah repeatedly urged Elisha to stay behind, but each time, Elisha responded with unwavering resolve: "As surely as the Lord lives and as you live, I will not leave you" (2 Kings 2:2, 2:4, 2:6).

Their journey was not just a physical one but a journey of faith and preparation. Elijah, understanding the significance of his imminent departure, used these final moments to impart wisdom and guidance to Elisha. They discussed the challenges that lay ahead, the responsibilities of a prophet, and the importance of remaining faithful to God's calling. Elisha listened intently, absorbing every word, knowing that soon he would have to stand alone and lead the people of Israel.

As they approached the Jordan River, the company of prophets from Jericho watched from a distance. These prophets, aware of the special relationship between Elijah and Elisha, were also aware of the significant event about to unfold. There was a sense of reverence and awe as they witnessed these final moments between the great prophet Elijah and his devoted disciple Elisha.

# Elijah's Ascension to Heaven in a Whirlwind

The Jordan River, a symbol of transition and divine intervention in Israel's history, became the backdrop for one of the most dramatic and miraculous events in the Bible. Elijah, with Elisha by his side, took his cloak, rolled it up, and struck the water. The waters parted to the right and to the left, allowing the two prophets to cross on dry ground. This act of parting the Jordan echoed the miracles of Moses at the Red Sea and Joshua at the same river, underscoring the continuity of God's miraculous provision and intervention.

Once they crossed the Jordan, Elijah and Elisha continued their walk, deep in conversation. It was during this walk that Elijah asked Elisha a profound question: "Tell me, what can I do for you before I am taken from you?" (2 Kings 2:9). This question was not merely a test but an opportunity for Elisha to express his deepest desires and intentions regarding his future ministry. Elisha's response was immediate and bold: "Let me inherit a double portion of your spirit" (2 Kings 2:9).

Elisha's request for a double portion of Elijah's spirit was a humble recognition of the immense responsibility he was about to undertake. He sought the spiritual strength, wisdom, and power necessary to lead the people and fulfill God's prophetic mission. Elijah acknowledged the difficulty of the request but assured Elisha that if he witnessed his departure, his request would be granted.

As they continued walking and talking, suddenly a chariot of fire and horses of fire appeared, separating the two of them. Elijah was taken up to heaven in a whirlwind (2 Kings 2:11). This miraculous ascension was a divine affirmation of Elijah's life and ministry. It was a spectacular demonstration of God's power and presence, underscoring the importance of Elijah's role and the continuation of his mission through Elisha.

# Elisha Receives Elijah's Mantle and the Prophetic Spirit

Witnessing Elijah's ascension, Elisha cried out, "My father! My father! The chariots and horsemen of Israel!" (2 Kings 2:12). This cry was a profound expression of loss, respect, and recognition of the spiritual significance of the moment. The chariots and horsemen of Israel symbolized God's power and protection, and Elijah's departure marked a significant transition in the spiritual leadership of Israel.

Elisha picked up the cloak that had fallen from Elijah and stood on the bank of the Jordan. This cloak, which had once symbolized Elijah's prophetic authority, now signified the transfer of that authority to Elisha. With a mixture of faith and determination, Elisha struck the water with the cloak and cried out, "Where now is the Lord, the God of Elijah?" (2 Kings 2:14). The waters of the Jordan parted once again, confirming that the spirit of Elijah now rested upon Elisha.

This moment was a powerful affirmation of Elisha's new role. The miracle of the parting waters not only demonstrated God's continued presence and power but also established Elisha's prophetic authority in the eyes of the other prophets and the people of Israel. It was a sign that God had indeed granted Elisha the double portion of Elijah's spirit, equipping him for the challenges and responsibilities ahead.

As Elisha crossed back over the Jordan, the company of prophets from Jericho acknowledged that the spirit of Elijah now rested on Elisha. They bowed to the ground before him, recognizing his new role and the divine authority he now carried. This acknowledgment was crucial for Elisha as he stepped into his prophetic ministry, providing him with the support and recognition he needed to lead effectively.

## Bible Verse: 2 Kings 2:11

"As they were walking along and talking together, suddenly a chariot of fire and horses of fire appeared and separated the two of them, and Elijah went up to heaven in a whirlwind."

## Reflections on Elijah's Ascension

Elijah's ascension to heaven is one of the most remarkable events in biblical history. It signifies not only the end of Elijah's earthly ministry but also the beginning of a new chapter in God's plan for Israel. Elijah's life and ministry were characterized by bold faith, unwavering obedience, and powerful miracles. His ascension in a whirlwind, accompanied by chariots and horses of fire, is a fitting culmination of his extraordinary life.

This event highlights the continuity of God's work through successive generations. Elijah's mantle and prophetic spirit were passed on to Elisha, ensuring that God's messages and miracles would continue to be delivered to the people of Israel. This transfer of authority underscores the importance of mentorship, discipleship, and the preparation of future leaders in God's kingdom.

Elisha's request for a double portion of Elijah's spirit reflects his understanding of the immense responsibility he was about to undertake. His bold request and the subsequent granting of this request demonstrate the importance of seeking God's empowerment for the tasks He has called us to. Elisha's story is a powerful reminder that God equips and empowers those He calls, providing them with the spiritual resources they need to fulfill their mission.

# The Significance of the Chariot of Fire and Horses of Fire

The appearance of the chariot of fire and horses of fire is rich with symbolic meaning. In the ancient Near Eastern context, chariots and horses were symbols of military power and protection. Their fiery nature signifies divine presence and power, highlighting the supernatural aspect of Elijah's ascension. This imagery reinforces the idea that Elijah's ministry was under divine protection and that his departure was orchestrated by God Himself.

The chariot of fire and horses of fire also symbolize the transition of spiritual leadership. As Elijah was taken up to heaven, Elisha was left to continue the work. This dramatic scene underscores the divine approval of Elisha's new role and the continuity of God's prophetic mission. It serves as a reminder that God's work is not dependent on any one individual but is carried out through successive generations of faithful servants.

# Elisha's Prophetic Ministry Begins

With Elijah's ascension, Elisha's prophetic ministry began in earnest. The miraculous parting of the Jordan River was just the beginning of a series of miracles and acts of divine intervention that would characterize Elisha's ministry. Elisha's journey from disciple to prophet was marked by his unwavering faith, boldness, and reliance on God's power.

Elisha's first act as a prophet, parting the waters of the Jordan, was a powerful demonstration of his new authority. It signaled to the other prophets and the people of Israel that Elisha was now God's chosen instrument. This act of faith and power set the tone for Elisha's ministry, which would be marked by numerous miracles, including healing the sick, raising the dead, and providing for the needy.

Elisha's prophetic ministry was characterized by compassion and a deep concern for the people of Israel. He used his gifts and authority to serve others, demonstrating God's love and power in tangible ways. His ministry was a continuation of Elijah's, but it also had its unique aspects and challenges. Through it all, Elisha remained faithful to his calling, relying on the double portion of Elijah's spirit to guide and empower him.

# The Legacy of Elijah and Elisha

The legacy of Elijah and Elisha is a testament to the power of mentorship, faith, and divine calling. Elijah's boldness and faithfulness set a powerful example for Elisha, who in turn became a conduit of God's power and love. Their stories are intertwined, highlighting the continuity of God's work through successive generations.

Elijah's ascension and Elisha's subsequent ministry demonstrate that God's work is not confined to a single individual but is carried out through a community of faithful servants. The mantle of prophecy passed from Elijah to Elisha symbolizes the ongoing nature of God's mission and the importance of preparing future leaders to carry on this work.

The stories of Elijah and Elisha continue to inspire believers today. They remind us of the importance of faithfulness, boldness, and reliance on God's power. They encourage us to seek God's guidance and empowerment for the tasks He has called us to and to be prepared to pass on the mantle of leadership to future generations.

## Conclusion

Elijah's ascension to heaven in a whirlwind marks a pivotal moment in the history of Israel and the prophetic mission. It signifies the end of Elijah's earthly ministry and the beginning of Elisha's. The final moments between Elijah and Elisha, the dramatic ascension, and the transfer of the prophetic mantle are rich with spiritual significance and lessons for believers today.

Elisha's journey from disciple to prophet is a powerful testament to the importance of faith, commitment, and divine empowerment. His unwavering determination to stay with Elijah until the end, his bold request for a double portion of Elijah's spirit, and his immediate stepping into the prophetic role demonstrate the qualities that are essential for effective ministry.

The chariot of fire and horses of fire, the miraculous parting of the Jordan, and Elisha's subsequent ministry all highlight the continuity of God's work and the importance of preparing future leaders. Elijah's legacy continued through Elisha, and the impact of their ministries is felt to this day.

As we reflect on the story of Elijah's ascension and Elisha's prophetic calling, we are reminded of the importance of faithfulness, boldness, and reliance on God's power. We are encouraged to seek God's guidance and empowerment for the tasks He has called us to and to be prepared to pass on the mantle of leadership to future generations. Through their example, we see the transformative power of God's call and the impact of faithful obedience on the world.

# Chapter 4: The Waters of Jericho

## Elisha's First Miracle at Jericho

Elisha had crossed the Jordan River, carrying with him the mantle of Elijah and the double portion of his spirit. This event not only marked his official succession but also the beginning of his miraculous ministry. His first significant act as the leading prophet of Israel took place in Jericho, a city steeped in history and symbolism. Jericho was the first city that Joshua had conquered in the Promised Land, but it now faced a dire crisis that threatened its very existence.

The people of Jericho approached Elisha with a pressing concern. The city's water source, a spring that should have been a life-giving blessing, had become tainted and poisonous. This contamination rendered the land barren and unproductive, causing death and despair among the inhabitants. The irony was not lost on Elisha—the very source meant to sustain life was now causing destruction.

Elisha, filled with compassion and guided by the Spirit of the Lord, listened intently to the plight of the people. His heart went out to them, understanding that water was not just a physical necessity but also a symbol of spiritual vitality and God's provision. The situation in Jericho provided Elisha with an opportunity to demonstrate God's power and his own prophetic authority, establishing his role as a miracle worker and a healer.

## Healing the Barren and Poisonous Waters

Elisha's response to the crisis at Jericho was both immediate and decisive. He requested a new bowl and had it filled with salt. This request might have seemed peculiar to those present, but Elisha knew that salt had symbolic significance in the covenant between God and His people. Salt was a symbol of purification, preservation, and divine blessing. It represented the power of God to cleanse and restore.

With the bowl of salt in hand, Elisha went to the source of the contaminated spring. This act was deeply symbolic—by addressing the root of the problem, Elisha was demonstrating that true healing must begin at the source. Standing at the spring, Elisha threw the salt into the water and proclaimed, "This is what the LORD says: I have healed this water. Never again will it cause death or make the land unproductive" (2 Kings 2:21).

In that moment, the waters were miraculously healed. The poison was removed, and the spring was restored to its original, life-giving state. The transformation was immediate and complete. The people of Jericho witnessed the power of God at work through Elisha, and their faith was renewed. The barren land began to flourish once more, and the death that had plagued the community was replaced with life and productivity.

## The Transformation of Jericho's Land and Its Impact on the People

The healing of the waters of Jericho had far-reaching implications. It was not just a physical transformation but also a spiritual renewal for the people. The land that had been cursed with barrenness and death was now blessed with fertility and life. The people of Jericho experienced firsthand the power of God's intervention and the faithfulness of His promises.

The immediate impact on the land was evident. Crops began to grow, and the once barren fields turned green with vegetation. The people who had suffered from the poisonous water now found themselves with an abundance of clean, pure water. Livestock that had been dying off began to thrive again. The economic and social life of Jericho was revitalized, and hope was restored to the community.

On a deeper level, the miracle reinforced the people's faith in God and their trust in His prophet, Elisha. The transformation of the water served as a powerful testimony of God's mercy and His ability to bring life out of death. It reminded the people that God was intimately involved in their lives and that He could transform any situation, no matter how dire, through His divine power.

Elisha's miracle at Jericho also established his authority as a prophet in the eyes of the people. It showed that he was not only a successor to Elijah but also a powerful instrument of God's will. The people of Jericho now saw Elisha as a source of divine intervention and guidance, someone they could turn to in times of need. This miracle set the stage for the many other signs and wonders that Elisha would perform throughout his ministry.

## Bible Verse: 2 Kings 2:21

"Then he went out to the spring and threw the salt into it, saying, 'This is what the LORD says: I have healed this water. Never again will it cause death or make the land unproductive.'"

## Reflections on the Miracle of Jericho's Waters

The healing of the waters of Jericho is a profound story that carries significant lessons for believers today. It is a testament to God's power to transform and heal even the most desperate situations. The story highlights several key themes, including the importance of addressing issues at their source, the symbolic power of salt, and the impact of faith and divine intervention.

## Addressing Issues at Their Source

Elisha's decision to heal the waters by going directly to the source of the spring carries a powerful message. It teaches us that true healing and transformation often require addressing problems at their root. Superficial solutions may provide temporary relief, but lasting change comes from dealing with the underlying causes. In our own lives, we are called to examine the root of our struggles and seek God's guidance in addressing them.

## The Symbolic Power of Salt

Salt, in the context of this miracle, symbolizes purification, preservation, and covenant. Throughout the Bible, salt is used as a symbol of God's covenant with His people. It represents His commitment to purify and preserve those who are faithful to Him. Elisha's use of salt to heal the waters reminds us of the importance of purity and the transformative power of God's covenant. It encourages us to seek spiritual purification and to trust in God's promises.

# Faith and Divine Intervention

The miracle at Jericho underscores the importance of faith and the reality of divine intervention. The people of Jericho were in a desperate situation, but they turned to Elisha, believing in his ability to bring about change through God's power. Their faith was rewarded with a miraculous transformation. This story reminds us that no situation is beyond God's ability to heal and transform. It calls us to trust in His power and to seek His intervention in our lives.

# Elisha's Role as a Prophet and Healer

Elisha's first miracle at Jericho established him as a prophet and healer in the eyes of the people. It demonstrated his deep compassion and his willingness to use his gifts to serve others. This miracle set the tone for Elisha's ministry, which would be marked by numerous acts of healing, provision, and divine intervention. Elisha's role as a prophet was not just about delivering messages but also about bringing tangible expressions of God's love and power to the people.

# The Broader Impact of the Miracle

The healing of the waters had a ripple effect on the entire community of Jericho. It transformed not only the physical environment but also the social and economic life of the city. The miracle brought hope and renewal to a people who had been living in despair. It serves as a reminder that God's interventions are holistic, impacting every aspect of our lives. When God heals, He brings restoration that goes beyond the immediate issue, touching every part of our existence.

### Conclusion

The miracle of the waters of Jericho is a powerful testament to God's ability to bring life and healing to even the most desperate situations. Elisha's act of healing the contaminated spring demonstrates the importance of addressing issues at their source, the symbolic power of salt, and the impact of faith and divine intervention. This miracle established Elisha's authority as a prophet and healer, setting the stage for his ministry of miracles and divine guidance.

As we reflect on this story, we are reminded of the transformative power of God's intervention in our lives. We are encouraged to address the root causes of our struggles, to seek spiritual purification, and to trust in God's covenant promises. The miracle of Jericho's waters calls us to have faith in God's power to heal and transform any situation, no matter how dire. It invites us to experience the holistic restoration that comes from God's intervention, touching every part of our lives with His love and power.

## The Historical and Cultural Context of Jericho

To fully appreciate the significance of Elisha's miracle at Jericho, it is important to understand the historical and cultural context of the city. Jericho was one of the oldest inhabited cities in the world, with a rich history dating back thousands of years. Known as the "City of Palms," Jericho was strategically located near the Jordan River, making it a key trade and cultural center in the region.

Jericho held a significant place in Israel's history. It was the first city conquered by Joshua and the Israelites when they entered the Promised Land (Joshua 6). The dramatic fall of Jericho's walls, brought about by God's miraculous intervention, marked a major turning point in Israel's conquest of Canaan. This historical backdrop adds a layer of meaning to Elisha's miracle, connecting his act of healing with the city's legacy of divine intervention and transformation.

The people of Jericho, living with the memory of their city's miraculous past, would have been particularly receptive to Elisha's prophetic ministry. Their faith in God's ability to intervene in their lives was rooted in the stories of their ancestors. This historical context helps us understand the significance of Elisha's act of healing the waters—an act that not only addressed a pressing physical need but also reinforced the city's legacy of divine miracles.

# The Role of Prophets in Ancient Israel

Elisha's miracle at Jericho highlights the important role that prophets played in ancient Israel. Prophets were not only messengers of God's word but also agents of His power and presence. They served as intermediaries between God and the people, delivering messages of warning, guidance, and hope. Prophets were often called to perform miraculous acts as signs of God's authority and as demonstrations of His power.

Elisha, as the successor to Elijah, carried on this prophetic tradition with great faithfulness and power. His acts of healing, provision, and divine intervention were tangible expressions of God's care for His people. The miracle at Jericho was one of many such acts that established Elisha's authority and demonstrated his role as a true prophet of God.

Prophets in ancient Israel were also seen as defenders of social justice and advocates for the marginalized. They spoke out against corruption, idolatry, and injustice, calling the people back to faithfulness to God. Elisha's ministry, while marked by miraculous acts, also included strong messages of justice and righteousness. His role as a prophet was multifaceted, encompassing both spiritual guidance and practical intervention.

# The Symbolism of Water in the Bible

Water holds deep symbolic significance throughout the Bible, often representing life, purification, and divine blessing. From the creation narrative, where God's Spirit hovered over the waters (Genesis 1:2), to the life-giving rivers described in the visions of Ezekiel (Ezekiel 47) and Revelation (Revelation 22), water is consistently portrayed as a source of life and renewal.

In the context of Elisha's miracle, the contaminated spring represented a corruption of this life-giving symbol. The healing of the waters restored not only the physical source of life for the people of Jericho but also the spiritual symbolism of water as a divine blessing. Elisha's act of purifying the water with salt reinforced the connection between God's covenant and the life-giving power of water.

The use of water in baptism, a central sacrament in the Christian faith, also draws on this rich symbolism. Baptism represents purification, rebirth, and initiation into the community of faith. Elisha's miracle at Jericho can be seen as a precursor to this sacramental understanding of water, highlighting its role as a medium of divine grace and transformation.

## Lessons for Contemporary Believers

The story of Elisha's healing of the waters of Jericho offers several important lessons for contemporary believers. It challenges us to examine the sources of our own struggles and to seek God's intervention in addressing them. It reminds us of the power of faith and the importance of trusting in God's ability to transform even the most desperate situations.

One key lesson is the importance of addressing issues at their source. Just as Elisha went to the spring to heal the waters, we are called to examine the root causes of our problems and seek God's guidance in addressing them. This may involve a process of spiritual purification, repentance, and renewal. By confronting the underlying issues, we open ourselves to God's transformative power.

The story also highlights the symbolic power of salt as a purifying and preserving agent. In the New Testament, Jesus calls His followers the "salt of the earth" (Matthew 5:13), emphasizing their role in preserving and purifying the world. As believers, we are called to live lives of purity and to be agents of God's grace and truth in the world.

Faith and divine intervention are central themes in the story of Jericho's waters. The people of Jericho turned to Elisha in faith, believing in his ability to bring about change through God's power. Their faith was rewarded with a miraculous transformation. This reminds us that no situation is beyond God's ability to heal and transform. We are called to trust in His power and to seek His intervention in our lives.

Finally, the story underscores the importance of holistic restoration. God's interventions are not limited to addressing immediate needs but extend to every aspect of our lives. The healing of the waters brought physical, economic, and social renewal to Jericho. Similarly, God's work in our lives touches every part of our existence, bringing comprehensive restoration and blessing.

### Conclusion

The miracle of the waters of Jericho is a powerful testament to God's ability to bring life and healing to even the most desperate situations. Elisha's act of healing the contaminated spring demonstrates the importance of addressing issues at their source, the symbolic power of salt, and the impact of faith and divine intervention. This miracle established Elisha's authority as a prophet and healer, setting the stage for his ministry of miracles and divine guidance.

As we reflect on this story, we are reminded of the transformative power of God's intervention in our lives. We are encouraged to address the root causes of our struggles, to seek spiritual purification, and to trust in God's covenant promises. The miracle of Jericho's waters calls us to have faith in God's power to heal and transform any situation, no matter how dire. It invites us to experience the holistic restoration that comes from God's intervention, touching every part of our lives with His love and power.

Through the historical and cultural context of Jericho, the role of prophets in ancient Israel, and the rich symbolism of water in the Bible, we gain a deeper understanding of the significance of this miracle. Elisha's ministry serves as a powerful example of faithfulness, compassion, and divine empowerment. His story encourages us to seek God's guidance and to be instruments of His grace and truth in the world.

In our own lives, we are called to be agents of transformation, addressing the root causes of issues, living lives of purity, and trusting in God's power to bring about change. The story of Elisha and the waters of Jericho challenges us to examine our own sources of struggle and to seek God's intervention in bringing about holistic restoration and blessing. Through faith and divine intervention, we can experience the transformative power of God's grace in every aspect of our lives.

# Chapter 5: The Curse of the Mocking Youths

## Elisha's Encounter with Mocking Youths at Bethel

After Elisha's dramatic initiation into prophetic ministry with the healing of the waters at Jericho, he continued his journey, spreading God's word and performing miracles. As he moved through the land, the people began to recognize him as Elijah's successor, and his reputation as a man of God grew. However, his journey was not without challenges and opposition, as evidenced by his encounter with a group of mocking youths at Bethel.

Bethel was a significant city in the religious history of Israel. It was a place where Jacob had a vision of a ladder reaching to heaven, and where he later set up an altar to God. However, by the time of Elisha, Bethel had become a center of idolatrous worship, a place where the people had turned away from the true worship of God. The spiritual decay of Bethel set the stage for the confrontation between Elisha and the mocking youths.

As Elisha approached Bethel, a group of young boys came out of the city and began to mock him. They jeered at him, saying, "Get out of here, baldy! Get out of here, baldy!" (2 Kings 2:23). The term "baldy" was a derogatory reference to Elisha's appearance, and the mocking was not merely about his physical traits but was an attack on his prophetic office and, by extension, on God Himself. The youths' behavior reflected the broader spiritual and moral decline of the city.

The mocking of Elisha by the youths was not a harmless act of childish mischief; it was a serious affront to God's appointed servant. In the culture of ancient Israel, respect for elders and especially for prophets was deeply ingrained. Prophets were seen as representatives of God, and to mock a prophet was to mock God. The behavior of the youths demonstrated a profound disrespect for divine authority and highlighted the moral and spiritual corruption that had taken root in Bethel.

# The Curse and the Attack by Bears

Elisha's response to the mocking was swift and severe. He turned around, looked at the youths, and called down a curse on them in the name of the LORD. Immediately, two bears came out of the woods and mauled forty-two of the boys (2 Kings 2:24). This dramatic and violent event served as a stark warning to the people of Bethel and to all of Israel about the consequences of disrespecting God's prophets and rejecting divine authority.

The curse and the subsequent attack by the bears can be difficult to understand from a modern perspective. It raises questions about the nature of God's justice and the severity of the punishment. However, in the context of ancient Israel, this event carried significant theological and moral implications. It was a powerful reminder of the seriousness of sin and the importance of reverence for God and His representatives.

The attack by the bears was not an act of senseless violence but a divinely orchestrated event that served several purposes. First, it affirmed Elisha's authority as a prophet and demonstrated that he was truly empowered by God. The immediate and supernatural nature of the punishment showed that Elisha's curse was backed by divine power, reinforcing his position as Elijah's successor.

Second, the event served as a warning to the people of Bethel and to all of Israel. It underscored the importance of respecting God's prophets and adhering to divine authority. The mocking youths represented the broader societal rejection of God's ways, and their punishment was a call to repentance and a return to faithfulness. It was a clear message that God would not tolerate blatant disrespect and rebellion.

Third, the event highlighted the seriousness of sin and the need for accountability. The youths' mocking was not a trivial matter but a manifestation of deeper spiritual issues. Their punishment served as a sobering reminder that actions have consequences and that God's justice is both real and immediate. It called the people to reflect on their own behavior and to turn back to God.

# Reflection on Respect for God's Prophets and Authority

The encounter between Elisha and the mocking youths at Bethel provides a profound lesson on the importance of respect for God's prophets and divine authority. Throughout the Bible, prophets were appointed by God to deliver His messages, guide His people, and call them to repentance. They were often met with resistance, mockery, and persecution, yet their role was crucial in the spiritual life of Israel.

The story of the mocking youths and their punishment highlights several key themes related to respect for God's prophets and authority.

## 1. The Role of Prophets as God's Representatives

Prophets in ancient Israel were not merely religious figures but were seen as direct representatives of God. They were chosen and empowered by God to speak His words, perform miracles, and guide the people. Disrespecting a prophet was equivalent to disrespecting God. The punishment of the mocking youths underscores the gravity of this offense and the importance of honoring God's chosen servants.

## 2. The Seriousness of Sin and Disrespect

The mocking of Elisha by the youths was a manifestation of deeper spiritual and moral issues within the community. It reflected a lack of reverence for God and a rejection of His authority. The severe punishment served as a stark reminder of the seriousness of sin and the need for accountability. It called the people to examine their own behavior and attitudes towards God and His representatives.

## 3. The Importance of Reverence and Respect

Respect for God, His prophets, and divine authority is a recurring theme throughout the Bible. It is a fundamental aspect of the covenant relationship between God and His people. The story of the mocking youths highlights the importance of reverence and respect in maintaining a healthy spiritual relationship with God. It calls believers to honor God's representatives and to approach Him with humility and reverence.

## 4. The Consequences of Rejecting Divine Authority

The punishment of the mocking youths serves as a warning about the consequences of rejecting divine authority. It demonstrates that actions have consequences and that God's justice is real and immediate. This event calls believers to reflect on their own attitudes and behavior towards God and His representatives and to recognize the importance of submitting to divine authority.

## Bible Verse: 2 Kings 2:24

"He turned around, looked at them and called down a curse on them in the name of the LORD. Then two bears came out of the woods and mauled forty-two of the boys."

## The Broader Context of Elisha's Ministry

Elisha's encounter with the mocking youths at Bethel was one of many significant events in his ministry. As Elijah's successor, Elisha carried on the prophetic mission with great faithfulness and power. His ministry was marked by numerous miracles, acts of healing, and powerful demonstrations of God's authority. The story of the mocking youths fits into a broader narrative of Elisha's role as a prophet and the challenges he faced.

Elisha's ministry was characterized by a deep compassion for the people and a commitment to God's justice. He performed miracles that brought healing and provision, such as the purification of the waters at Jericho and the multiplication of the widow's oil. At the same time, he confronted sin and rebellion with boldness and decisiveness, as seen in the encounter with the mocking youths.

The story of the mocking youths also highlights the tension between true worship and idolatry in Israel. Bethel had become a center of idolatrous worship, and the mocking of Elisha reflected the spiritual decay of the city. Elisha's curse and the subsequent punishment served as a call to repentance and a return to true worship. It was a reminder that God demanded reverence and obedience and that idolatry would not be tolerated.

# Theological Implications of the Event

The encounter with the mocking youths and their punishment raises important theological questions about God's justice, mercy, and the role of prophets. It challenges us to consider the nature of divine punishment and the balance between justice and mercy in God's dealings with humanity.

## 1. God's Justice and Mercy

The severity of the punishment meted out to the mocking youths can be difficult to reconcile with the concept of a loving and merciful God. However, it is important to understand that God's justice and mercy are not mutually exclusive. God's justice demands accountability for sin, while His mercy offers forgiveness and restoration to those who repent. The punishment of the youths served as a warning and a call to repentance, emphasizing the seriousness of sin and the need for reverence.

## 2. The Role of Prophets as Instruments of God's Justice

Prophets in ancient Israel often served as instruments of God's justice, delivering messages of warning and calling the people to repentance. Elisha's curse on the mocking youths was an expression of God's justice, demonstrating the consequences of disrespect and rebellion. It highlighted the prophet's role in upholding divine authority and maintaining the spiritual integrity of the community.

## 3. The Importance of Reverence and Fear of the Lord

The story of the mocking youths underscores the importance of reverence and fear of the Lord. Throughout the Bible, the fear of the Lord is described as the beginning of wisdom and the foundation of a healthy spiritual relationship with God. The punishment of the youths served as a stark reminder of the need for reverence and respect in our relationship with God and His representatives.

## 4. The Call to Repentance and Restoration

While the punishment of the mocking youths was severe, it also served as a call to repentance and restoration. It highlighted the consequences of sin and the need for the people to turn back to God. The event was a reminder that God's justice is accompanied by His call to repentance and His desire for restoration and reconciliation with His people.

# Lessons for Contemporary Believers

The story of Elisha and the mocking youths at Bethel offers several important lessons for contemporary believers. It challenges us to reflect on our attitudes towards God, His representatives, and divine authority. It calls us to examine the seriousness of sin and the importance of reverence and respect in our spiritual lives.

## 1. Respect for Spiritual Leaders

The story highlights the importance of respecting spiritual leaders who are called by God to guide and shepherd His people. Disrespecting spiritual leaders is not just a personal affront but an act of rebellion against God's authority. We are called to honor and support those who have been entrusted with spiritual leadership and to recognize the divine authority they carry.

## 2. The Seriousness of Sin

The punishment of the mocking youths serves as a sobering reminder of the seriousness of sin and the consequences of rebellion against God. It challenges us to examine our own behavior and attitudes towards God and His representatives. We are called to take sin seriously and to seek God's forgiveness and transformation in our lives.

## 3. The Importance of Reverence

Reverence for God and His representatives is a foundational aspect of our spiritual relationship with Him. The story of the mocking youths calls us to cultivate an attitude of reverence and humility in our approach to God. It reminds us that God is holy and worthy of our utmost respect and honor.

## 4. The Call to Repentance

The event at Bethel serves as a call to repentance for the people of Israel and for us today. It underscores the need to turn away from sin and to seek God's forgiveness and restoration. Repentance is not just about avoiding punishment but about restoring our relationship with God and aligning our lives with His will.

### Conclusion

The story of Elisha and the mocking youths at Bethel is a powerful and challenging narrative that highlights the importance of respect for God's prophets and divine authority. The encounter and the subsequent punishment serve as a stark reminder of the seriousness of sin and the need for reverence in our relationship with God.

Elisha's ministry was marked by a deep commitment to God's justice and compassion for the people. His encounter with the mocking youths at Bethel was one of many significant events that demonstrated his prophetic authority and the power of God at work through him. The story challenges us to reflect on our own attitudes towards God, His representatives, and the importance of reverence and respect in our spiritual lives.

As we consider the broader context of Elisha's ministry, the theological implications of the event, and the lessons for contemporary believers, we are reminded of the transformative power of God's justice and mercy. The story calls us to examine the root causes of our struggles, to seek spiritual purification, and to trust in God's covenant promises.

Through the story of Elisha and the mocking youths, we see the importance of respecting spiritual leaders, taking sin seriously, cultivating reverence, and responding to the call to repentance. It is a story that invites us to experience the transformative power of God's grace and to live lives that honor Him in every aspect.

# Chapter 6: The Widow's Oil

## A Widow in Debt Seeks Elisha's Help

In the ancient world of Israel, the life of a widow was fraught with challenges and uncertainties. Widows were among the most vulnerable members of society, often facing dire poverty and social marginalization. The story of the widow and the miraculous multiplication of oil is a powerful testament to God's compassion and provision for those in desperate need. This narrative unfolds against the backdrop of Elisha's prophetic ministry, showcasing his role as a conduit of God's mercy and power.

The widow in this story was not just any widow; she was the wife of a member of the company of prophets, a man who had served faithfully but had passed away, leaving his family in a precarious situation. The widow approached Elisha with a heart heavy with anxiety and desperation. Her late husband had left behind debts that she had no means to repay, and the creditor was threatening to take her two sons as slaves to settle the debt. In ancient Israel, such actions, though harsh, were not uncommon, and the widow found herself at the mercy of circumstances beyond her control.

As she stood before Elisha, the widow poured out her plight, hoping for a miracle. Her plea was simple yet profound, revealing both her dire circumstances and her faith in the power of God working through His prophet. "Your servant my husband is dead," she said, "and you know that he revered the LORD. But now his creditor is coming to take my two boys as his slaves" (2 Kings 4:1). Her words carried the weight of her desperation and her hope that Elisha, as a man of God, could intercede on her behalf.

Elisha, moved by her plight, responded with compassion and practical wisdom. He asked her, "How can I help you? Tell me, what do you have in your house?" (2 Kings 4:2). The widow's response highlighted the extent of her poverty: "Your servant has nothing there at all," she said, "except a small jar of olive oil" (2 Kings 4:2). This seemingly insignificant possession would become the focal point of a divine miracle, demonstrating God's ability to use the smallest resources to bring about abundant provision.

# The Miracle of the Multiplied Oil

Elisha's instructions to the widow were both simple and profound. He told her, "Go around and ask all your neighbors for empty jars. Don't ask for just a few. Then go inside and shut the door behind you and your sons. Pour oil into all the jars, and as each is filled, put it to one side" (2 Kings 4:3-4). The prophet's command required the widow to take a step of faith, acting in obedience to a seemingly illogical instruction. Gathering empty jars from her neighbors was an act of faith, trusting that God would indeed provide in a miraculous way.

The widow and her sons went out and collected as many empty jars as they could find. Their willingness to follow Elisha's instructions without fully understanding how the miracle would unfold was a testament to their faith. Returning home, they shut the door as instructed, creating a private space for the miracle to occur. This act of closing the door can be seen as a symbolic gesture, indicating a separation from the doubting world and an intimate encounter with God's provision.

With her sons by her side, the widow began to pour the small amount of oil she had into the first empty jar. To her astonishment, the oil continued to flow, filling one jar after another. As each jar was filled, her sons brought her another, and the oil did not cease. This miraculous multiplication of oil was a tangible demonstration of God's limitless provision and His power to transform a seemingly insignificant resource into an abundant supply.

The Bible verse captures the culmination of this miracle: "When all the jars were full, she said to her son, 'Bring me another one.' But he replied, 'There is not a jar left.' Then the oil stopped flowing" (2 Kings 4:6). The miracle was perfectly timed and measured; it provided exactly what was needed, no more and no less. The cessation of the oil's flow once the last jar was filled emphasized that God's provision is always sufficient and meets the exact needs of His people.

# The Widow's Faith and God's Provision

The widow's faith played a crucial role in the unfolding of this miracle. Her willingness to trust Elisha's instructions, gather empty jars, and pour out the oil despite her initial doubts and fears demonstrated a profound reliance on God's power. Her faith was not passive; it was active and involved taking concrete steps in obedience to the prophet's command. This active faith is a model for believers, showing that trust in God often requires action and participation in His promises.

God's provision in this story is not only a testament to His compassion but also a reflection of His faithfulness to those who serve Him. The widow's husband had been a faithful servant of God, and even in death, his family experienced the divine care and provision that he had believed in during his lifetime. This narrative reassures believers that God sees their needs and is both willing and able to provide for them in miraculous ways.

The impact of the miracle extended beyond the immediate need for debt repayment. With the jars of oil, the widow was able to sell the surplus, ensuring long-term financial stability for herself and her sons. Elisha's final instruction to her was, "Go, sell the oil and pay your debts. You and your sons can live on what is left" (2 Kings 4:7). This outcome highlights God's concern for the holistic well-being of His people, addressing both immediate crises and long-term needs.

The story of the widow's oil also underscores the importance of community and mutual support. The neighbors who provided the empty jars played an indirect but vital role in the miracle. Their willingness to contribute to the widow's need created the conditions for God's provision to manifest. This element of the story encourages believers to be attentive to the needs of those around them and to participate in acts of generosity and support, knowing that they may be facilitating God's work in ways they do not fully understand.

## Bible Verse: 2 Kings 4:6

"When all the jars were full, she said to her son, 'Bring me another one.' But he replied, 'There is not a jar left.' Then the oil stopped flowing."

## Reflections on the Miracle of the Widow's Oil

The miracle of the multiplied oil is a profound demonstration of God's provision and a powerful lesson on faith, obedience, and community. It invites believers to reflect on the nature of divine provision and the ways in which God meets the needs of His people through both miraculous and ordinary means. Several key themes emerge from this story, offering insights and encouragement for contemporary believers.

## The Role of Faith in Experiencing God's Provision

The widow's faith was instrumental in the unfolding of the miracle. Her willingness to follow Elisha's seemingly illogical instructions, gather empty jars, and pour out the little oil she had demonstrated a deep trust in God's power. This active faith is a crucial component of experiencing God's provision. It involves taking steps of obedience, even when the outcome is uncertain, and trusting that God will fulfill His promises.

The widow's faith was not passive but required action. This dynamic interplay between faith and action is a recurring theme in the Bible. James 2:17 reminds us that "faith by itself, if it is not accompanied by action, is dead." The widow's story exemplifies the truth that genuine faith often involves taking concrete steps in response to God's word, creating the conditions for His provision to manifest.

## God's Compassion and Care for the Vulnerable

The story of the widow's oil is a powerful reminder of God's compassion and care for the most vulnerable members of society. Widows, orphans, and the poor are frequently mentioned in the Bible as those deserving of special care and protection. God's intervention in the widow's situation highlights His deep concern for those who are marginalized and in desperate need.

This narrative reassures believers that God sees their struggles and is intimately aware of their needs. It encourages those who are facing difficult circumstances to trust in God's compassion and provision. Psalm 68:5 describes God as "a father to the fatherless, a defender of widows." The miracle of the widow's oil is a tangible expression of this divine care, offering hope and encouragement to all who find themselves in vulnerable situations.

# The Importance of Obedience and Action

Elisha's instructions to the widow required her to take specific actions in obedience to God's word. Gathering empty jars and pouring out the oil were acts of faith that set the stage for the miracle. This aspect of the story highlights the importance of obedience and action in experiencing God's provision. Believers are called to respond to God's instructions with faith and action, trusting that He will work through their obedience to bring about His purposes.

Obedience is a recurring theme in the Bible, often linked to experiencing God's blessings. Deuteronomy 28:1-2 promises that if God's people fully obey His commands, they will experience His blessings in every area of their lives. The widow's story illustrates this principle, showing that obedience, even in seemingly small and insignificant actions, can lead to miraculous outcomes.

# Community and Mutual Support

The miracle of the widow's oil also underscores the importance of community and mutual support. The neighbors who provided the empty jars played a crucial role in the miracle, even though they may not have fully understood the significance of their actions. This element of the story highlights the interconnectedness of the community and the ways in which God's provision often involves the cooperation and support of others.

Believers are called to be attentive to the needs of those around them and to participate in acts of generosity and support. Galatians 6:2 encourages us to "carry each other's burdens, and in this way you will fulfill the law of Christ." The widow's story illustrates how small acts of kindness and support can facilitate God's work and create the conditions for His provision to manifest.

# The Sufficiency and Timeliness of God's Provision

The cessation of the oil's flow once the last jar was filled emphasizes that God's provision is always sufficient and timely. The miracle provided exactly what was needed to meet the widow's immediate and long-term needs, no more and no less. This aspect of the story reassures believers that God's provision is perfectly timed and measured to meet their needs.

Philippians 4:19 promises that "God will meet all your needs according to the riches of his glory in Christ Jesus." The widow's story exemplifies this truth, demonstrating that God's provision is not just about abundance but also about meeting specific needs in the right measure and at the right time. It encourages believers to trust in God's perfect timing and sufficiency in all circumstances.

## Conclusion

The story of the widow's oil is a powerful testament to God's provision, compassion, and faithfulness. It highlights the crucial role of faith, obedience, and community in experiencing God's blessings and offers profound lessons for contemporary believers. The widow's active faith, her willingness to follow Elisha's instructions, and the miraculous multiplication of the oil demonstrate the transformative power of God's intervention.

As we reflect on this story, we are encouraged to cultivate an active faith that responds to God's word with obedience and action. We are reminded of God's deep compassion and care for the vulnerable and are called to trust in His provision in all circumstances. The importance of community and mutual support is emphasized, inviting us to participate in acts of generosity and kindness that facilitate God's work in the lives of others.

Through the lens of this narrative, we see the sufficiency and timeliness of God's provision, reassuring us that He knows our needs and will meet them according to His perfect wisdom and timing. The miracle of the widow's oil calls us to a deeper trust in God's power and faithfulness, inspiring us to live lives marked by faith, obedience, and compassion.

# The Historical and Cultural Context

To fully appreciate the significance of the widow's story, it is important to understand the historical and cultural context of ancient Israel. Widows in ancient Israel were often left without means of support upon the death of their husbands. In a patriarchal society, where men were the primary providers, the loss of a husband could leave a widow destitute and vulnerable to exploitation.

The law of Moses included provisions for the protection and care of widows, reflecting God's concern for the most vulnerable members of society.

Deuteronomy 24:19-21, for example, commanded the Israelites to leave some of the harvest for widows, orphans, and foreigners. Despite these provisions, widows often faced significant challenges, especially when unscrupulous creditors sought to exploit their vulnerable situation.

The widow in this story faced the added pressure of an impending threat to her sons, who were at risk of being taken as slaves to settle the debt. This practice, though harsh, was permitted under the law, and it placed the widow in an incredibly desperate situation. Her approach to Elisha was not just a request for financial help but a plea for the preservation of her family and her future.

## The Role of Prophets in Providing Social Justice

Elisha's response to the widow's plight highlights the role of prophets in advocating for social justice and providing practical help to those in need. Prophets in ancient Israel were not only spiritual leaders but also social reformers who spoke out against injustice and oppression. They were called to defend the rights of the poor and marginalized and to ensure that the community lived according to God's laws of justice and compassion.

Elisha's intervention on behalf of the widow reflects this prophetic mission. By performing the miracle of the multiplied oil, Elisha addressed the immediate financial crisis and prevented the enslavement of the widow's sons. This act of compassion and justice underscored the prophet's role as a defender of the vulnerable and a conduit of God's provision.

The story challenges contemporary believers to consider the ways in which they can advocate for social justice and support those who are vulnerable and in need. It calls for a holistic approach to ministry that addresses both spiritual and practical needs, following the example of the prophets who combined their spiritual authority with acts of compassion and justice.

## The Symbolism of Oil in the Bible

Oil holds significant symbolic meaning in the Bible, often representing the Holy Spirit, anointing, and divine blessing. In ancient Israel, oil was used in religious ceremonies for anointing priests, kings, and prophets, signifying their consecration and empowerment by God. Oil was also a valuable commodity, used for cooking, lighting lamps, and medicinal purposes.

The miracle of the multiplied oil in the widow's story carries rich symbolic significance. It represents God's abundant provision and His ability to transform a small, seemingly insignificant resource into an abundant supply. The continuous flow of oil until all the jars were filled symbolizes the limitless nature of God's blessings and His ability to meet every need.

In the New Testament, oil is often associated with the Holy Spirit and the anointing of believers for ministry and service. The miracle of the widow's oil can be seen as a foreshadowing of the outpouring of the Holy Spirit, who empowers and equips believers for their mission. It reminds us that God's provision is not limited to material needs but includes spiritual empowerment and anointing for service.

# Lessons for Contemporary Believers

The story of the widow's oil offers several important lessons for contemporary believers, encouraging them to trust in God's provision, take steps of faith and obedience, and support those in need.

## 1. Trusting in God's Provision

The widow's story is a powerful reminder of God's faithfulness and His ability to provide for His people in miraculous ways. Believers are encouraged to trust in God's provision, even in the face of seemingly insurmountable challenges. The narrative reassures us that God sees our needs and is both willing and able to meet them according to His perfect wisdom and timing.

## 2. Taking Steps of Faith and Obedience

The widow's active faith and obedience to Elisha's instructions were crucial in the unfolding of the miracle. This aspect of the story challenges believers to take concrete steps of faith and obedience in response to God's word. It reminds us that faith often involves action and participation in God's promises, creating the conditions for His provision to manifest.

## 3. Supporting Those in Need

The role of the neighbors in providing empty jars highlights the importance of community and mutual support. Believers are called to be attentive to the needs of those around them and to participate in acts of generosity and support. By doing so, they create the conditions for God's work and facilitate His provision in the lives of others.

## 4. Recognizing the Sufficiency of God's Provision

The cessation of the oil's flow once all the jars were filled emphasizes that God's provision is always sufficient and perfectly timed. Believers are encouraged to trust in the sufficiency of God's provision, knowing that He will meet their needs in the right measure and at the right time. This trust in God's sufficiency brings peace and confidence, even in challenging circumstances.

## 5. Embracing a Holistic Approach to Ministry

Elisha's intervention on behalf of the widow reflects a holistic approach to ministry that addresses both spiritual and practical needs. Believers are called to follow this example, combining their spiritual authority with acts of compassion and justice. This holistic approach ensures that ministry is comprehensive and transformative, meeting the needs of the whole person.

### Conclusion

The story of the widow's oil is a powerful testament to God's provision, compassion, and faithfulness. It highlights the crucial role of faith, obedience, and community in experiencing God's blessings and offers profound lessons for contemporary believers. The widow's active faith, her willingness to follow Elisha's instructions, and the miraculous multiplication of the oil demonstrate the transformative power of God's intervention.

As we reflect on this story, we are encouraged to cultivate an active faith that responds to God's word with obedience and action. We are reminded of God's deep compassion and care for the vulnerable and are called to trust in His provision in all circumstances. The importance of community and mutual support is emphasized, inviting us to participate in acts of generosity and kindness that facilitate God's work in the lives of others.

Through the lens of this narrative, we see the sufficiency and timeliness of God's provision, reassuring us that He knows our needs and will meet them according to His perfect wisdom and timing. The miracle of the widow's oil calls us to a deeper trust in God's power and faithfulness, inspiring us to live lives marked by faith, obedience, and compassion.

The historical and cultural context of ancient Israel, the role of prophets in advocating for social justice, and the rich symbolism of oil in the Bible all contribute to our understanding of this profound story. The widow's story challenges contemporary believers to trust in God's provision, take steps of faith and obedience, and support those in need, embracing a holistic approach to ministry that reflects God's compassion and justice.

In our own lives, we are called to be instruments of God's provision and compassion, supporting those who are vulnerable and creating the conditions for His miraculous work. The story of the widow's oil invites us to experience the transformative power of God's grace and to live lives that honor Him in every aspect.

# Chapter 7: The Shunammite Woman

## Elisha's Friendship with a Wealthy Shunammite Woman

Elisha's ministry was characterized by his deep compassion for people and his willingness to engage with them in their daily lives. One of the most remarkable relationships he formed was with a wealthy Shunammite woman and her family. This relationship not only highlights the prophet's influence but also underscores the themes of hospitality, faith, and divine blessing.

Shunem was a town in the region of Issachar, known for its fertile land and prosperous inhabitants. Among its residents was a notable woman of means who extended extraordinary hospitality to Elisha. She perceived that Elisha was a holy man of God and sought to honor him by providing for his needs whenever he passed through her town. This woman's initiative in reaching out to Elisha was the beginning of a profound and life-changing relationship.

The Shunammite woman, whose name is not mentioned in the biblical text, approached her husband with a proposal. "I know that this man who often comes our way is a holy man of God," she said. "Let's make a small room on the roof and put in it a bed and a table, a chair and a lamp for him. Then he can stay there whenever he comes to us" (2 Kings 4:9-10). Her suggestion was motivated by a genuine desire to support Elisha's ministry and offer him a place of rest and refuge.

Elisha accepted the woman's hospitality, and her home became a regular stop on his travels. The simple yet thoughtful provision of a room for Elisha reflected the Shunammite woman's deep respect and reverence for the prophet. It also created a space for meaningful interaction and spiritual connection. Elisha's friendship with the Shunammite woman and her family grew over time, marked by mutual respect and a shared commitment to God's work.

## The Blessing of a Son to the Barren Woman

Despite her wealth and status, the Shunammite woman carried a deep personal sorrow—she was barren and had no children. In ancient Israel, having children was considered a blessing from God and a sign of His favor. The absence of children was often perceived as a source of shame and unfulfilled potential. The Shunammite woman's barrenness was a silent sorrow that lay hidden beneath her outward prosperity.

One day, Elisha, moved by gratitude for the woman's hospitality, sought to repay her kindness. He called her to him and asked, "You have gone to all this trouble for us. Now, what can be done for you? Can we speak on your behalf to the king or the commander of the army?" (2 Kings 4:13). The woman's response was humble and content: "I have a home among my own people" (2 Kings 4:13). She did not seek favors or rewards, but Elisha's servant, Gehazi, revealed her secret longing: "She has no son, and her husband is old" (2 Kings 4:14).

Elisha then made a prophetic declaration that would change the woman's life forever. "About this time next year," Elisha said, "you will hold a son in your arms" (2 Kings 4:16). The Shunammite woman's initial reaction was one of disbelief mixed with hope. "No, my lord!" she objected. "Please, man of God, don't mislead your servant!" (2 Kings 4:16). Despite her doubts, the prophecy came to pass, and as Elisha had foretold, she conceived and gave birth to a son the following year.

The Bible verse encapsulates the fulfillment of Elisha's prophecy: "But the woman became pregnant, and the next year about that same time she gave birth to a son, just as Elisha had told her" (2 Kings 4:17). This miraculous birth was a testament to God's power and faithfulness, transforming the woman's sorrow into joy and her barrenness into fruitfulness.

## The Woman's Hospitality and Its Rewards

The story of the Shunammite woman is a powerful example of how acts of hospitality and kindness can lead to unexpected and profound blessings. Her decision to provide a place for Elisha was an expression of her faith and reverence for God. It created an opportunity for divine intervention in her life, leading to the miraculous birth of her son.

Hospitality is a recurring theme in the Bible, often associated with blessings and divine favor. In the New Testament, hospitality is described as a virtue that should be practiced by all believers. Hebrews 13:2 advises, "Do not forget to show hospitality to strangers, for by so doing some people have shown hospitality to angels without knowing it." The Shunammite woman's story exemplifies this principle, showing that hospitality can be a conduit for God's blessings.

The rewards of the Shunammite woman's hospitality extended beyond the birth of her son. Her relationship with Elisha continued to bring blessings and protection to her family. Years later, when her son fell ill and died suddenly, the Shunammite woman's faith and her connection to Elisha played a crucial role in his miraculous resurrection.

When her son died, the woman did not succumb to despair. Instead, she laid him on Elisha's bed in the room she had prepared for the prophet and set out to find Elisha. Her actions demonstrated her unwavering faith and her belief that Elisha, as a man of God, could intercede on her behalf. Her journey to find Elisha was marked by determination and hope.

When Elisha saw the Shunammite woman approaching, he immediately recognized her distress. "Run to meet her and ask her, 'Are you all right? Is your husband all right? Is your child all right?'" he instructed Gehazi (2 Kings 4:26). The woman's response was resolute: "Everything is all right" (2 Kings 4:26). Despite her anguish, she maintained her faith in Elisha's ability to bring about a miracle.

Upon reaching Elisha, she fell at his feet and expressed her deep sorrow and desperation. Elisha, moved by her faith and determination, sent Gehazi ahead with his staff to place on the boy's face. However, the boy did not awaken. Elisha then went to the house, shut the door, and prayed to the LORD. He stretched himself out on the boy, and the child's body began to warm. Elisha's persistence in prayer and his actions resulted in the boy's revival. The woman's faith and hospitality had once again led to a miraculous intervention.

## Bible Verse: 2 Kings 4:17

"But the woman became pregnant, and the next year about that same time she gave birth to a son, just as Elisha had told her."

# Reflections on the Story of the Shunammite Woman

The story of the Shunammite woman and Elisha is rich with lessons on faith, hospitality, and the blessings that come from honoring God and His servants. It highlights the transformative power of faith and the unexpected ways in which God can intervene in the lives of those who trust in Him.

## The Power of Hospitality

The Shunammite woman's decision to provide a room for Elisha was an act of genuine hospitality and reverence for God. Her willingness to go beyond the norm and create a dedicated space for the prophet reflects a deep sense of respect and devotion. This act of hospitality opened the door for divine blessings that she could not have anticipated.

Hospitality is a powerful expression of faith and love. It involves opening one's home and heart to others, creating a space for connection and care. In the context of the Shunammite woman's story, hospitality became a means through which God's blessings flowed. Her example challenges contemporary believers to practice hospitality with a generous and open heart, trusting that God can use their acts of kindness to bring about His purposes.

## Faith in Action

The Shunammite woman's story is also a testament to the power of faith in action. Her willingness to create a room for Elisha, her response to his prophecy, and her determined journey to find Elisha when her son died all demonstrate a proactive and resilient faith. She did not passively wait for miracles to happen but took concrete steps in alignment with her faith.

This active faith is a key theme throughout the Bible. James 2:17 states, "Faith by itself, if it is not accompanied by action, is dead." The Shunammite woman's actions exemplify this principle, showing that faith often requires taking steps that demonstrate trust in God's promises. Her story encourages believers to put their faith into action, taking steps that align with their trust in God's power and faithfulness.

## Divine Intervention and Blessing

The miraculous birth of the Shunammite woman's son and his subsequent resurrection highlight the theme of divine intervention and blessing. God's intervention in her life transformed her sorrow into joy and her barrenness into fruitfulness. These miracles were not just acts of compassion but also affirmations of God's power and faithfulness.

God's blessings often come in unexpected ways and through unexpected means. The Shunammite woman's story reminds believers that God is intimately aware of their needs and capable of intervening in miraculous ways. It encourages a posture of openness to God's blessings, trusting that He can bring about transformation even in the most challenging circumstances.

## The Role of Prophets and Divine Messengers

Elisha's role in the Shunammite woman's story underscores the importance of prophets and divine messengers in the biblical narrative. Prophets were not only spokespersons for God but also instruments of His power and provision. Elisha's interactions with the Shunammite woman highlight the prophet's role as a conduit of God's blessings and a source of spiritual support and guidance.

The story encourages believers to recognize and honor the role of spiritual leaders and divine messengers in their lives. These individuals often play a crucial role in guiding, supporting, and facilitating God's work. By honoring and supporting them, believers can create opportunities for divine blessings and intervention.

## Hospitality as a Virtue and Spiritual Practice

The Shunammite woman's hospitality is a powerful example of a virtue that is highly valued in both the Old and New Testaments. Hospitality involves welcoming others into one's home and life, creating a space for connection and care. It is a tangible expression of love and faith, reflecting God's own hospitality towards humanity.

In the New Testament, hospitality is described as a spiritual practice that should be embraced by all believers. Romans 12:13 encourages believers to "practice hospitality," and 1 Peter 4:9 advises, "Offer hospitality to one another without grumbling." The Shunammite woman's story exemplifies this virtue, showing how hospitality can create opportunities for divine blessings and transformation.

## Conclusion

The story of the Shunammite woman is a powerful narrative that highlights the themes of hospitality, faith, and divine blessing. Her relationship with Elisha, marked by genuine hospitality and mutual respect, created the conditions for miraculous interventions that transformed her life. The birth of her son and his subsequent resurrection were profound demonstrations of God's power and faithfulness.

As we reflect on this story, we are encouraged to practice hospitality with a generous and open heart, recognizing that our acts of kindness can be conduits for God's blessings. The Shunammite woman's active faith, her willingness to take concrete steps in alignment with her trust in God, challenges us to put our faith into action and to trust in God's power to bring about transformation.

The story also reminds us of the importance of honoring and supporting spiritual leaders and divine messengers, recognizing their crucial role in facilitating God's work. By creating spaces of hospitality and connection, we can participate in God's work and experience His blessings in unexpected and profound ways.

The Shunammite woman's story is a testament to the transformative power of faith, hospitality, and divine intervention. It invites us to live lives marked by generosity, faith, and openness to God's blessings, trusting that He can bring about transformation and fulfillment in ways we may not anticipate. Through her example, we see the profound impact of faith and hospitality, and the ways in which God's power and faithfulness can manifest in our lives.

# Chapter 8: The Resurrection of the Shunammite's Son

## The Sudden Death of the Shunammite's Son

The Shunammite woman's story is one of profound faith, generosity, and divine blessing. Her hospitality toward the prophet Elisha had resulted in the miraculous birth of a son, a fulfillment of Elisha's prophetic promise. However, this story takes a dramatic and heartbreaking turn with the sudden death of her beloved child, plunging the family into deep sorrow and testing the limits of their faith.

The boy, born as a miraculous answer to his mother's deepest longings, had grown into a lively and cherished member of the family. His presence was a constant reminder of God's faithfulness and the blessings that had come from their association with Elisha. One day, while the boy was out in the fields with his father, he suddenly cried out, "My head! My head!" (2 Kings 4:19). Alarmed, his father instructed a servant to carry the boy back to his mother.

The Shunammite woman held her son on her lap, trying to comfort him, but by noon, the boy had died. The abruptness of his illness and the swiftness of his death were devastating. Her joy turned to sorrow, and her heart was shattered by this unexpected tragedy. However, her response to this crisis was marked by remarkable composure and unwavering faith.

Instead of succumbing to despair, the Shunammite woman laid her son's lifeless body on the bed in Elisha's room—the very room she had prepared for the prophet. This act of faith indicated her belief that Elisha, as a man of God, could intercede on her behalf and that her son's story was not yet over. She then shut the door and set out to find Elisha, determined to bring him back to her home.

## Elisha's Journey to Revive the Child

The Shunammite woman's journey to find Elisha was fueled by a desperate hope and a steadfast faith in the prophet's ability to perform a miracle. She instructed her servant to saddle a donkey and urged him to make haste: "Lead on; don't slow down for me unless I tell you" (2 Kings 4:24). Her urgency and determination were evident, as she would not rest until she had reached Elisha and secured his help.

Elisha was at Mount Carmel when the woman arrived. Seeing her approaching from a distance, Elisha recognized her and sent his servant Gehazi to meet her and inquire about her well-being. Gehazi's questions—"Are you all right? Is your husband all right? Is your child all right?"—were met with a resolute but brief response: "Everything is all right" (2 Kings 4:26). Despite her grief, the Shunammite woman's answer reflected her unwavering faith in the outcome of her mission.

Upon reaching Elisha, the woman fell at his feet, overwhelmed by emotion. Gehazi attempted to push her away, but Elisha intervened, sensing the depth of her distress. "Leave her alone! She is in bitter distress, but the LORD has hidden it from me and has not told me why" (2 Kings 4:27). The woman then revealed the heartbreaking truth: "Did I ask you for a son, my lord? Didn't I tell you, 'Don't raise my hopes'?" (2 Kings 4:28). Her words expressed both her anguish and her implicit faith in Elisha's power to change the situation.

Moved by her plea, Elisha immediately took action. He instructed Gehazi to take his staff and go ahead to the Shunammite's house. "If you meet anyone, do not greet him, and if anyone greets you, do not answer. Lay my staff on the boy's face" (2 Kings 4:29). Gehazi obeyed, but the Shunammite woman insisted that Elisha himself come with her: "As surely as the LORD lives and as you live, I will not leave you" (2 Kings 4:30). Her determination to have Elisha personally intervene underscores her deep trust in him.

Elisha and the Shunammite woman traveled back to her home together. Upon arriving, they found that Gehazi had already placed the staff on the boy's face, but there was no sign of life. The boy remained lifeless, and the situation seemed hopeless to all but the Shunammite woman and Elisha.

## The Miraculous Restoration of Life

Elisha's next actions were driven by a combination of faith, persistence, and reliance on God's power. He entered the room where the boy lay, shut the door behind him, and prayed to the LORD. This moment of private intercession highlighted Elisha's dependence on God for the miracle that was needed.

After praying, Elisha did something extraordinary. He stretched himself out upon the boy, placing his mouth on the boy's mouth, his eyes on the boy's eyes, and his hands on the boy's hands. As he lay upon the boy, the child's body began to warm (2 Kings 4:34). Elisha then got up and walked back and forth in the room, perhaps seeking further guidance and strength from God. He returned to the boy and stretched out upon him once more.

The Bible verse captures the climactic moment: "Elisha turned away and walked back and forth in the room and then got on the bed and stretched out upon him once more. The boy sneezed seven times and opened his eyes" (2 Kings 4:35). The boy's sneezing was a clear sign of life returning, and when he opened his eyes, it was a moment of profound joy and relief. God had answered Elisha's prayers and performed a miracle, restoring life to the Shunammite woman's son.

Elisha called Gehazi and instructed him to summon the boy's mother. When she came in, Elisha said, "Take your son" (2 Kings 4:36). The Shunammite woman fell at Elisha's feet in gratitude and then took her son in her arms. Her faith had been rewarded, and her sorrow turned to joy. The restoration of her son's life was a testament to God's power and the efficacy of faith and prayer.

# The Family's Gratitude and Reflections on the Miracle

The resurrection of the Shunammite woman's son had a profound impact on her family and on all who heard of the miracle. It was a powerful demonstration of God's ability to bring life out of death and a testament to the faithfulness of His promises. The family's gratitude was immense, and their faith in God was deeply strengthened.

The Shunammite woman's story serves as a powerful reminder of the importance of faith, persistence in prayer, and the recognition of God's sovereignty. Her journey from despair to joy underscores the transformative power of divine intervention and the role of faith in experiencing God's miracles.

## Bible Verse: 2 Kings 4:35

"Elisha turned away and walked back and forth in the room and then got on the bed and stretched out upon him once more. The boy sneezed seven times and opened his eyes."

# Reflections on the Resurrection of the Shunammite's Son

The resurrection of the Shunammite woman's son is a powerful narrative that highlights several key themes, including the power of faith, the importance of persistence in prayer, and the miraculous intervention of God. This story provides profound insights and encouragement for contemporary believers, reminding them of the transformative power of divine intervention.

## The Power of Faith and Determination

The Shunammite woman's faith and determination are central to this narrative. Despite the devastating loss of her son, she did not succumb to despair but instead took decisive action to seek Elisha's help. Her journey to find the prophet, her insistence that he come with her, and her unwavering belief in his ability to perform a miracle all demonstrate a profound and active faith.

This story challenges believers to cultivate a faith that is both resilient and proactive. The Shunammite woman's example encourages us to trust in God's power and to take concrete steps in alignment with our faith, even in the face of seemingly insurmountable challenges. Her determination to seek out Elisha and bring him back to her home is a powerful reminder of the importance of persistence and action in our spiritual lives.

## The Role of Persistence in Prayer

Elisha's actions in the room where the boy lay lifeless highlight the importance of persistence in prayer. Elisha's initial prayer, followed by his physical actions, and then more prayer, reflect a deep reliance on God and a refusal to give up.

The prophet's willingness to continue praying and seeking God's intervention until the boy was restored to life underscores the power of persistent prayer.

This aspect of the story resonates with the teaching of Jesus in the New Testament, where He encourages His followers to persist in prayer. In Luke 18:1, Jesus tells His disciples a parable to show them that they should always pray and not give up. Elisha's persistence in prayer serves as a powerful example of this principle, reminding believers that God honors and responds to persistent, faith-filled prayer.

## Divine Intervention and Miracles

The miraculous resurrection of the Shunammite woman's son is a testament to God's power and His ability to intervene in even the most hopeless situations. This story underscores the belief that God is not limited by natural laws and can perform miracles that defy human understanding. The boy's revival from death to life is a powerful reminder of God's sovereignty and His ability to bring about miraculous transformation.

For contemporary believers, this story offers hope and encouragement. It reassures them that no situation is beyond God's ability to redeem and transform. The Shunammite woman's story challenges us to trust in God's power to work miracles in our own lives and to maintain faith in His ability to intervene in extraordinary ways.

## The Role of Prophets and Spiritual Leaders

Elisha's role in this narrative highlights the importance of prophets and spiritual leaders in facilitating God's work. As a prophet, Elisha was a conduit of God's power and a source of spiritual guidance and support for the Shunammite woman and her family. His willingness to respond to the woman's plea and his actions in reviving the boy demonstrate the crucial role that spiritual leaders play in supporting and interceding for their communities.

This story encourages believers to recognize and honor the role of spiritual leaders in their lives. It underscores the importance of seeking out and supporting those who are called to guide and intercede on behalf of the community. By valuing and supporting spiritual leaders, believers can create an environment where God's work can flourish and where miraculous interventions can occur.

# The Transformative Power of God's Intervention

The resurrection of the Shunammite woman's son had a transformative impact on her family and on the broader community. It was a powerful demonstration of God's ability to bring life out of death and to transform sorrow into joy. This miracle not only restored the boy's life but also deepened the family's faith and gratitude, reinforcing their trust in God's faithfulness.

This narrative invites believers to reflect on the transformative power of God's intervention in their own lives. It encourages them to recognize and celebrate the ways in which God has brought about transformation and healing, even in the most challenging circumstances. The story of the Shunammite woman and her son serves as a testament to the profound impact of God's miraculous work and the enduring power of faith.

## Conclusion

The story of the resurrection of the Shunammite woman's son is a powerful and moving narrative that highlights the themes of faith, persistence in prayer, and divine intervention. The sudden death of the boy and his miraculous revival through Elisha's intercession underscore the transformative power of God's work and the importance of trust and action in experiencing His miracles.

As we reflect on this story, we are encouraged to cultivate a resilient and proactive faith, to persist in prayer, and to trust in God's power to bring about miraculous transformation. The Shunammite woman's example challenges us to take decisive action in alignment with our faith and to seek God's intervention with unwavering determination.

Elisha's role in this narrative underscores the importance of spiritual leaders and their crucial role in facilitating God's work. By recognizing and honoring the role of prophets and spiritual leaders, believers can create an environment where God's work can flourish and where miraculous interventions can occur.

The resurrection of the Shunammite woman's son is a testament to the transformative power of God's intervention and the profound impact of faith. It invites us to trust in God's power to work miracles in our own lives and to celebrate the ways in which He has brought about transformation and healing. Through this story, we see the enduring power of faith and the limitless potential of God's miraculous work.

# Chapter 9: The Poisoned Stew

## A Famine in the Land and the Prophet's Community

During the time of Elisha, the land of Israel faced various challenges, one of which was a severe famine. This famine struck the land hard, affecting the livelihoods of many and putting communities at risk of starvation. The prophet's community, known as the company of prophets, was also impacted by this crisis. These were the disciples of Elisha, young men who were training under him to serve as prophets and spiritual leaders in Israel.

The famine was a period of intense hardship and testing. It was a time when faith and reliance on God were crucial for survival. The scarcity of food meant that the community had to make do with whatever resources they could find, often leading to creative but sometimes risky solutions to meet their basic needs. This period of deprivation set the stage for a miraculous intervention that would highlight Elisha's role as a prophet and God's continuing care for His people.

Elisha, as the leader of this prophetic community, was deeply concerned about the well-being of his disciples. His responsibility was not only to teach and guide them spiritually but also to ensure their physical survival during these difficult times. The famine tested the resilience of the community and their faith in God's provision. It was in this context that the incident of the poisoned stew occurred, demonstrating both the danger of desperation and the power of divine intervention.

## The Incident of the Poisoned Stew

One day, while the famine was at its peak, Elisha instructed his servant to prepare a meal for the prophets. "Put on the large pot and cook some stew for these men," he said (2 Kings 4:38). This was a routine task, but the famine had made the availability of safe and nutritious food a significant challenge. The men had to forage for ingredients, often relying on wild plants and herbs to supplement their meals.

One of the young prophets went out into the fields to gather herbs. In his search, he found a wild vine and picked some of its gourds. Not recognizing the plant, he brought the gourds back, cut them up, and added them to the pot of stew. The ingredients were unfamiliar, but the desperate circumstances made it necessary to use whatever could be found.

As the stew cooked, it filled the air with a tantalizing aroma, and the hungry men eagerly awaited their meal. However, as soon as they began to eat, they realized something was terribly wrong. The taste was bitter and unpleasant, and almost immediately, they felt the effects of the poison. They cried out to Elisha in panic, "Man of God, there is death in the pot!" (2 Kings 4:40). Their exclamation revealed their fear and the severity of the situation.

The poisoned stew was a direct threat to the lives of the prophets. The wild gourds were likely from the colocynth plant, known for its toxic properties. Consuming even a small amount could cause severe illness or death. The community's reliance on foraged food during the famine had inadvertently led them to a life-threatening crisis. The fear and urgency of their cry to Elisha underscored the gravity of the situation and their dependence on the prophet for a solution.

## Elisha's Intervention and the Stew's Purification

Elisha's response to the crisis was calm and decisive. He did not panic or express fear, but instead, he sought divine guidance to address the deadly situation. Elisha called for some flour and, without hesitation, threw it into the pot. "Get some flour," he said. "Put it into the pot and serve it to the people to eat" (2 Kings 4:41). This act was both practical and symbolic, representing Elisha's faith in God's ability to purify and heal.

The use of flour to neutralize the poison was not based on any known scientific principle but was an act of faith and a prophetic gesture. It was a symbolic act, much like Moses' use of a piece of wood to sweeten the bitter waters of Marah (Exodus 15:25). By adding flour to the stew, Elisha demonstrated his reliance on God's power to bring about healing and restoration.

Elisha's instruction to serve the stew to the people after adding the flour was a bold expression of faith. It required the prophets to trust in Elisha's prophetic authority and in God's ability to perform a miracle. The act of serving and consuming the stew after the intervention was a testament to their collective faith in God's provision and protection.

Miraculously, the flour purified the stew, rendering it safe to eat. The Bible verse captures the outcome: "Elisha said, 'Get some flour.' He put it into the pot and said, 'Serve it to the people to eat.' And there was nothing harmful in the pot" (2 Kings 4:41). This divine intervention not only saved the lives of the prophets but also reinforced their faith in God's care and in Elisha's prophetic leadership.

# The Community's Gratitude and Reflection

The miraculous purification of the poisoned stew had a profound impact on the prophetic community. It was a powerful demonstration of God's presence and protection amidst the trials of the famine. The prophets' gratitude for Elisha's intervention was immense, and their faith in God's provision was strengthened. This incident became a significant testimony of God's ability to turn a potentially deadly situation into a demonstration of His power and mercy.

The community's reflection on this event likely included several key lessons:

## 1. Faith in God's Provision:

The famine was a period of scarcity and desperation, but the incident of the poisoned stew reinforced the belief that God could provide even in the most challenging circumstances. The community learned that their trust in God's provision was well-placed, as He had the power to purify and transform what seemed harmful into something life-giving.

## 2. The Importance of Discernment:

The young prophet's unintentional gathering of poisonous gourds highlighted the need for discernment, especially during times of crisis. The community learned the importance of seeking wisdom and guidance, not just relying on their own understanding, particularly when making decisions that could affect their well-being.

## 3. The Role of Prophetic Leadership:

Elisha's calm and faith-filled response to the crisis underscored the importance of prophetic leadership. His reliance on God's guidance and his decisive action provided a model for the community. The incident reinforced the respect and trust that the prophets had in Elisha's leadership and his close relationship with God.

## 4. The Power of Symbolic Actions:

The use of flour to purify the stew was a symbolic act that demonstrated the power of faith and prophetic gestures. The community saw firsthand that God could work through simple, symbolic actions to bring about miraculous results. This lesson deepened their understanding of the ways in which God could manifest His power.

## Bible Verse: 2 Kings 4:41

"Elisha said, 'Get some flour.' He put it into the pot and said, 'Serve it to the people to eat.' And there was nothing harmful in the pot."

# Reflections on the Incident of the Poisoned Stew

The story of the poisoned stew is rich with lessons on faith, reliance on God's provision, and the role of prophetic leadership. It highlights the importance of trusting in God's ability to purify and heal, even in the most dire circumstances. Several key themes emerge from this narrative, offering insights and encouragement for contemporary believers.

## Faith in God's Provision and Protection

The incident of the poisoned stew underscores the importance of faith in God's provision and protection. The community of prophets faced a life-threatening crisis, but their trust in Elisha's prophetic leadership and in God's power brought about a miraculous solution. This story challenges believers to trust in God's provision, even in times of scarcity and desperation.

The community's reliance on foraged food during the famine was a practical necessity, but it also exposed them to risks. The poisoned stew incident highlights the dangers that can arise in desperate situations. However, it also demonstrates that God's protection is available, and He can intervene to neutralize harm and provide for His people. This lesson encourages believers to have faith in God's ability to protect and provide, even when resources are limited.

## The Role of Prophetic Leadership

Elisha's role in the incident of the poisoned stew is a powerful example of prophetic leadership. His calm and decisive response to the crisis, his reliance on God's guidance, and his symbolic use of flour to purify the stew all demonstrate the qualities of a true prophet. Elisha's actions provided a model for the community, reinforcing their faith in his leadership and in God's power.

Prophetic leadership involves more than just delivering messages from God; it includes guiding, protecting, and interceding for the community. Elisha's intervention in the poisoned stew incident highlights the importance of prophetic leaders who are attuned to God's guidance and capable of taking decisive action in times of crisis. This story encourages believers to honor and support their spiritual leaders, recognizing the vital role they play in guiding and protecting the community.

## The Power of Symbolic Actions

The use of flour to purify the stew is a key element of the story, highlighting the power of symbolic actions. In the Bible, symbolic actions often serve as tangible expressions of faith and divine intervention. Elisha's act of adding flour to the stew was not based on any scientific principle but was a prophetic gesture that demonstrated his faith in God's ability to heal and purify.

This aspect of the story encourages believers to recognize the significance of symbolic actions in their spiritual lives. Whether it is the use of anointing oil, the laying on of hands, or other symbolic acts, these actions can serve as powerful expressions of faith and conduits for God's power. The story of the poisoned stew reminds believers that God can work through simple, symbolic actions to bring about miraculous results.

# The Importance of Discernment

The young prophet's unintentional gathering of poisonous gourds highlights the importance of discernment, especially during times of crisis. The community's reliance on foraged food during the famine made them vulnerable to potentially harmful mistakes. This incident underscores the need for wisdom and discernment in making decisions, particularly when the stakes are high.

Believers are encouraged to seek God's guidance and wisdom in all areas of their lives, especially when facing challenging circumstances. The story of the poisoned stew serves as a reminder that discernment is crucial and that God can provide the wisdom needed to navigate difficult situations safely.

# Divine Intervention and Miracles

The miraculous purification of the poisoned stew is a powerful demonstration of divine intervention and God's ability to perform miracles. The community's desperate situation was transformed into a testimony of God's power and care. This story encourages believers to trust in God's ability to intervene miraculously in their lives and to bring about healing and restoration.

Miracles are a testament to God's sovereignty and His compassion for His people. The incident of the poisoned stew reminds believers that no situation is beyond God's ability to redeem and transform. It challenges them to maintain faith in God's power to work miracles and to seek His intervention in times of need.

## Conclusion

The story of the poisoned stew is a powerful narrative that highlights the themes of faith, prophetic leadership, and divine intervention. The famine and the resulting desperation of the prophetic community set the stage for a life-threatening crisis that was miraculously resolved through Elisha's intervention. The purification of the poisoned stew is a testament to God's power and His care for His people.

As we reflect on this story, we are encouraged to cultivate a deep faith in God's provision and protection, even in times of scarcity and desperation. The community's reliance on Elisha's prophetic leadership and their trust in his ability to perform a miracle highlight the importance of honoring and supporting spiritual leaders who guide and protect the community.

The use of symbolic actions, such as Elisha's addition of flour to the stew, underscores the power of faith-filled gestures in experiencing God's intervention. Believers are encouraged to recognize the significance of symbolic actions in their spiritual lives and to use them as tangible expressions of faith.

The importance of discernment is also a key lesson from this story. The young prophet's mistake in gathering poisonous gourds highlights the need for wisdom and guidance, especially during challenging times. Believers are reminded to seek God's wisdom and discernment in all areas of their lives.

Finally, the miraculous purification of the poisoned stew serves as a powerful reminder of God's ability to intervene and perform miracles. Believers are encouraged to trust in God's power to bring about healing and restoration, even in the most dire circumstances. The story of the poisoned stew challenges us to maintain faith in God's sovereignty and to seek His intervention in times of need.

The incident of the poisoned stew is a testament to the transformative power of faith and divine intervention. It invites us to trust in God's provision, honor prophetic leadership, recognize the power of symbolic actions, seek discernment, and believe in the possibility of miracles. Through this story, we see the enduring power of faith and the limitless potential of God's miraculous work.

# Chapter 10: Feeding a Hundred Men

## A Man Brings Elisha an Offering of Food

In the time of Elisha, the land of Israel was enduring a period of hardship and famine. Resources were scarce, and many people were struggling to find enough food to sustain themselves. Despite these challenging circumstances, acts of generosity and faith continued to shine through. One such act involved a man from Baal Shalishah who brought an offering of food to Elisha, demonstrating his faith and trust in God's provision.

The man brought twenty loaves of barley bread and some heads of new grain. Barley loaves were considered the bread of the poor, as barley was less expensive and less desirable than wheat. However, this man's offering was significant, given the famine and scarcity of resources. It was an act of faith and devotion, showing his recognition of Elisha as a prophet of God and his willingness to share what little he had.

Elisha's reputation as a man of God and a prophet had spread far and wide. People knew that Elisha performed miracles and that he was closely connected to God. Bringing an offering to Elisha was seen as a way to honor God and seek His blessing. The man from Baal Shalishah's decision to bring food to Elisha during a time of famine was a testament to his faith and his desire to support the prophet and his community.

When the man presented the offering to Elisha, it was clear that the food was intended to be a blessing. However, the amount of food seemed insufficient to meet the needs of the large group of prophets who were with Elisha. The community of prophets, often referred to as the "sons of the prophets," relied on Elisha for leadership and sustenance. The offering of twenty loaves of barley bread and some new grain, though generous, appeared inadequate to feed the entire group.

## The Miracle of the Multiplied Loaves and Grain

Elisha, however, saw an opportunity for God to demonstrate His power and provision. He instructed his servant to distribute the food to the people. "Give it to the people to eat," Elisha said (2 Kings 4:42). This command must have seemed perplexing to the servant, given the meager amount of food in comparison to the number of men present.

The servant expressed his concern, questioning how such a small amount of food could possibly feed a hundred men. "How can I set this before a hundred men?" he asked (2 Kings 4:43). The servant's question was practical and reflected the reality of the situation. From a human perspective, it seemed impossible for the limited offering to meet the needs of so many.

Elisha, confident in God's ability to provide, responded with a prophetic declaration: "Give it to the people to eat. For this is what the LORD says: They will eat and have some left over" (2 Kings 4:43). Elisha's words echoed the divine assurance that God's provision would not only be sufficient but also abundant. The promise of having leftovers emphasized the abundance of God's provision, surpassing the immediate needs of the people.

With faith in Elisha's words and the power of God, the servant obeyed and set the food before the people. As the food was distributed, a miraculous event occurred. The small offering of twenty loaves of barley bread and some new grain was multiplied to feed all the men present. Each man ate until he was satisfied, and just as Elisha had prophesied, there was food left over.

The Bible verse captures this miraculous event: "His servant said, 'How can I set this before a hundred men?' But Elisha answered, 'Give it to the people to eat. For this is what the LORD says: They will eat and have some left over.' Then he set it before them, and they ate and had some left over, according to the word of the LORD" (2 Kings 4:43-44). This miracle was a powerful demonstration of God's ability to provide abundantly, even in the face of scarcity and need.

## The Feeding of a Hundred Men and the Lesson of God's Abundance

The feeding of the hundred men through the multiplication of the loaves and grain is a profound testament to God's abundant provision and the importance of faith. This miracle, performed by Elisha, prefigures similar miracles in the New Testament, such as Jesus feeding the multitudes with loaves and fish. It highlights several key lessons about God's nature and the way He cares for His people.

## 1. God's Abundant Provision

One of the central themes of this miracle is God's abundant provision. Despite the scarcity of resources during the famine, God demonstrated His ability to provide more than enough for His people. The small offering of barley loaves and grain was multiplied to feed a hundred men, with leftovers remaining. This miracle underscores the idea that God's provision is not limited by human constraints or scarcity. He is able to provide abundantly, exceeding our expectations and meeting our needs in ways that surpass human understanding.

This lesson is a source of comfort and encouragement for believers facing challenging circumstances. It reassures them that God is aware of their needs and is fully capable of providing for them in abundance. The miracle of the multiplied loaves and grain encourages believers to trust in God's provision and to have faith that He will supply their needs, even when resources appear limited.

## 2. The Power of Faith and Obedience

Elisha's faith in God's ability to perform the miracle was unwavering. Despite the servant's practical concerns about the insufficiency of the food, Elisha's confidence in God's promise did not waver. His command to distribute the food was an act of faith, trusting that God would fulfill His word.

The servant's obedience, despite his initial doubts, was also crucial in the unfolding of the miracle. By following Elisha's instructions and distributing the food, the servant participated in the miracle and witnessed firsthand the power of God's provision. This aspect of the story highlights the importance of faith and obedience in experiencing God's miracles. Believers are encouraged to trust in God's promises and to act in faith, even when circumstances seem impossible.

## 3. The Significance of Small Offerings

The man from Baal Shalishah's offering, though small in quantity, became the catalyst for a miraculous demonstration of God's abundance. This story illustrates that even small offerings, when given in faith and with a generous heart, can be used by God to accomplish great things. The multiplication of the loaves and grain shows that God can take what little we have and transform it into something much greater.

This lesson encourages believers to offer what they have to God, regardless of the size or perceived value. God honors the heart behind the offering and has the power to multiply and use it for His purposes. The story of the multiplied loaves and grain reminds believers that their contributions, no matter how small, can be used by God to bring about significant blessings.

## 4. The Importance of Community and Sharing

The feeding of the hundred men through the multiplication of the loaves and grain also underscores the importance of community and sharing. The prophetic community, gathered around Elisha, relied on each other for support and sustenance during the famine. The man's offering was intended to bless the entire community, and the miracle ensured that everyone was fed.

This story highlights the value of sharing resources and supporting one another, especially during times of need. It encourages believers to be generous and to contribute to the well-being of their community. By sharing what they have, believers create an environment where God's blessings can be experienced collectively. The miracle of the multiplied loaves and grain serves as a reminder that God's provision often flows through acts of generosity and communal support.

## 5. A Foretaste of Greater Miracles

The miracle of feeding the hundred men with a small offering prefigures similar miracles in the New Testament, particularly Jesus' feeding of the multitudes. In the Gospels, Jesus performed miracles where He multiplied loaves and fish to feed thousands of people. These miracles echo the themes of God's abundant provision, the power of faith, and the significance of small offerings.

Elisha's miracle serves as a foreshadowing of the greater miracles to come, pointing to the continuity of God's work throughout the Scriptures. It highlights the consistent nature of God's care for His people and His ability to provide for their needs in miraculous ways. The feeding of the hundred men with barley loaves and grain connects the Old and New Testaments, showing that God's character and His provision remain constant.

# Bible Verse: 2 Kings 4:43-44

"His servant said, 'How can I set this before a hundred men?' But Elisha answered, 'Give it to the people to eat. For this is what the LORD says: They will eat and have some left over.' Then he set it before them, and they ate and had some left over, according to the word of the LORD."

# Reflections on the Feeding of the Hundred Men

The story of the feeding of the hundred men through the multiplication of the loaves and grain is rich with spiritual insights and lessons that are relevant for contemporary believers. It highlights the themes of God's abundant provision, the power of faith and obedience, the significance of small offerings, the importance of community and sharing, and the foreshadowing of greater miracles.

## God's Abundant Provision

The central theme of this miracle is God's abundant provision. Despite the scarcity of resources during the famine, God demonstrated His ability to provide more than enough for His people. The small offering of barley loaves and grain was multiplied to feed a hundred men, with leftovers remaining. This miracle underscores the idea that God's provision is not limited by human constraints or scarcity. He is able to provide abundantly, exceeding our expectations and meeting our needs in ways that surpass human understanding.

For contemporary believers, this lesson is a source of comfort and encouragement. It reassures them that God is aware of their needs and is fully capable of providing for them in abundance. The miracle of the multiplied loaves and grain encourages believers to trust in God's provision and to have faith that He will supply their needs, even when resources appear limited. It challenges them to look beyond their immediate circumstances and to trust in God's ability to provide in miraculous ways.

## The Power of Faith and Obedience

Elisha's unwavering faith in God's ability to perform the miracle is a powerful example for believers. Despite the servant's practical concerns about the insufficiency of the food, Elisha's confidence in God's promise did not waver. His command to distribute the food was an act of faith, trusting that God would fulfill His word.

The servant's obedience, despite his initial doubts, was also crucial in the unfolding of the miracle. By following Elisha's instructions and distributing the food, the servant participated in the miracle and witnessed firsthand the power of God's provision. This aspect of the story highlights the importance of faith and obedience in experiencing God's miracles. Believers are encouraged to trust in God's promises and to act in faith, even when circumstances seem impossible. The story challenges them to step out in faith and to trust in God's ability to work through their obedience.

## The Significance of Small Offerings

The man from Baal Shalishah's offering, though small in quantity, became the catalyst for a miraculous demonstration of God's abundance. This story illustrates that even small offerings, when given in faith and with a generous heart, can be used by God to accomplish great things. The multiplication of the loaves and grain shows that God can take what little we have and transform it into something much greater.

This lesson encourages believers to offer what they have to God, regardless of the size or perceived value. God honors the heart behind the offering and has the power to multiply and use it for His purposes. The story of the multiplied loaves and grain reminds believers that their contributions, no matter how small, can be used by God to bring about significant blessings. It challenges them to be generous and to trust that God can use their offerings to make a difference.

## The Importance of Community and Sharing

The feeding of the hundred men through the multiplication of the loaves and grain underscores the importance of community and sharing. The prophetic community, gathered around Elisha, relied on each other for support and sustenance during the famine. The man's offering was intended to bless the entire community, and the miracle ensured that everyone was fed.

This story highlights the value of sharing resources and supporting one another, especially during times of need. It encourages believers to be generous and to contribute to the well-being of their community. By sharing what they have, believers create an environment where God's blessings can be experienced collectively. The miracle of the multiplied loaves and grain serves as a reminder that God's provision often flows through acts of generosity and communal support. It challenges believers to look out for one another and to support each other in times of need.

## A Foretaste of Greater Miracles

The miracle of feeding the hundred men with a small offering prefigures similar miracles in the New Testament, particularly Jesus' feeding of the multitudes. In the Gospels, Jesus performed miracles where He multiplied loaves and fish to feed thousands of people. These miracles echo the themes of God's abundant provision, the power of faith, and the significance of small offerings.

Elisha's miracle serves as a foreshadowing of the greater miracles to come, pointing to the continuity of God's work throughout the Scriptures. It highlights the consistent nature of God's care for His people and His ability to provide for their needs in miraculous ways. The feeding of the hundred men with barley loaves and grain connects the Old and New Testaments, showing that God's character and His provision remain constant.

For contemporary believers, this connection reinforces the idea that God's care and provision are timeless and unchanging. It encourages them to see the continuity of God's work and to trust in His ability to provide, just as He has done throughout history. The story of the multiplied loaves and grain challenges believers to look forward with hope and to trust in God's ongoing care and provision.

### Conclusion

The story of the feeding of the hundred men through the multiplication of the loaves and grain is a powerful narrative that highlights the themes of God's abundant provision, the power of faith and obedience, the significance of small offerings, the importance of community and sharing, and the foreshadowing of greater miracles. It serves as a testament to God's ability to provide abundantly and to transform scarcity into abundance.

As we reflect on this story, we are encouraged to cultivate a deep faith in God's provision and to trust in His ability to provide for our needs, even in times of scarcity and desperation. The miracle of the multiplied loaves and grain challenges us to step out in faith, to be obedient to God's instructions, and to trust in His promises.

The significance of small offerings is a key lesson from this story. It encourages us to offer what we have to God, knowing that He can use even the smallest contributions to accomplish great things. The story of the multiplied loaves and grain reminds us that our offerings, no matter how small, can be used by God to bring about significant blessings.

The importance of community and sharing is another crucial lesson from this story. It challenges us to be generous and to support one another, especially during times of need. By sharing what we have, we create an environment where God's blessings can be experienced collectively.

Finally, the miracle of feeding the hundred men with a small offering prefigures similar miracles in the New Testament and reinforces the continuity of God's work throughout the Scriptures. It reminds us that God's care and provision are timeless and unchanging, and it encourages us to trust in His ongoing care and provision.

The story of the feeding of the hundred men through the multiplication of the loaves and grain is a powerful testament to the enduring power of faith and the limitless potential of God's miraculous work. It invites us to trust in God's provision, to be generous and supportive of one another, and to look forward with hope, trusting in God's ongoing care and provision. Through this story, we see the consistent nature of God's character and His ability to provide for His people in miraculous ways.

# Chapter 11: Naaman's Healing

## Naaman, a Syrian Commander, Seeks Healing for His Leprosy

Naaman was a man of great stature and importance in the kingdom of Aram (modern-day Syria). As a commander of the army, he was highly regarded by his king and respected by his soldiers. His military prowess and strategic acumen had led to numerous victories, securing his position as a powerful and influential figure. Despite his accomplishments and status, Naaman was afflicted with a severe and debilitating condition: leprosy.

Leprosy, a term used in the Bible to describe a range of skin diseases, was a condition that not only affected one's physical health but also carried significant social stigma. Those afflicted with leprosy were often ostracized and considered unclean, leading to isolation and shame. For Naaman, a man accustomed to respect and authority, the disease was a source of profound personal anguish and humiliation.

In Naaman's household, there was a young Israelite girl who had been taken captive during one of Aram's raids into Israel. This girl served Naaman's wife, and despite her own circumstances, she expressed compassion for her master. Seeing his suffering, she told her mistress about a prophet in Samaria who could heal Naaman. "If only my master would see the prophet who is in Samaria! He would cure him of his leprosy" (2 Kings 5:3).

The girl's faith and boldness sparked hope in Naaman and his household. Clinging to the possibility of a cure, Naaman approached his king and relayed the girl's message. The king of Aram, valuing his commander and desperate for his recovery, readily agreed to send Naaman to Israel. He provided Naaman with a letter to the king of Israel, requesting that he facilitate the healing of his commander.

Armed with the letter and accompanied by a significant entourage, Naaman set out for Israel. He carried with him lavish gifts of silver, gold, and fine garments, intending to offer them as payment for his healing. The journey to Israel was marked by a mixture of hope and apprehension, as Naaman sought a cure for a condition that had plagued him for so long.

Upon arriving in Israel, Naaman presented the letter to the king. The king of Israel, however, was deeply distressed by the request, fearing it was a ploy to provoke conflict. "Am I God? Can I kill and bring back to life? Why does this fellow send someone to me to be cured of his leprosy?" the king exclaimed (2 Kings 5:7). The king's reaction revealed his lack of faith and understanding of the prophet's power.

## Elisha's Instructions to Wash in the Jordan River

When Elisha, the man of God, heard of the king's distress, he sent a message, offering a solution and calming the king's fears. "Why have you torn your robes? Have the man come to me and he will know that there is a prophet in Israel" (2 Kings 5:8). Elisha's confidence in God's power and his role as a prophet was unwavering.

Naaman, along with his horses and chariots, proceeded to Elisha's house. Expecting a grand gesture or elaborate ritual, Naaman was surprised when Elisha did not even come out to greet him. Instead, Elisha sent a messenger with simple yet specific instructions: "Go, wash yourself seven times in the Jordan, and your flesh will be restored and you will be cleansed" (2 Kings 5:10).

The simplicity of Elisha's instructions contrasted sharply with Naaman's expectations. He had anticipated a dramatic display of power, perhaps involving the prophet calling on the name of the LORD, waving his hand over the spot, and curing the leprosy. Naaman's pride and sense of self-importance were challenged by the humble directive to wash in the Jordan River, a body of water he deemed inferior to the rivers of Damascus.

Furious and insulted, Naaman turned away in a rage, exclaiming, "I thought that he would surely come out to me and stand and call on the name of the LORD his God, wave his hand over the spot and cure me of my leprosy. Are not Abana and Pharpar, the rivers of Damascus, better than any of the waters of Israel? Couldn't I wash in them and be cleansed?" (2 Kings 5:11-12). His reaction revealed his struggle with pride and his resistance to the simplicity of God's method.

However, Naaman's servants approached him with humility and reason, appealing to his desire for healing. They said, "My father, if the prophet had told you to do some great thing, would you not have done it? How much more, then, when he tells you, 'Wash and be cleansed'!" (2 Kings 5:13). Their words penetrated Naaman's anger, prompting him to reconsider Elisha's instructions.

## Naaman's Healing, His Conversion, and the Lesson of Humility and Faith

Overcoming his pride and skepticism, Naaman decided to follow Elisha's directive. He went down to the Jordan River, immersed himself seven times as instructed, and experienced a miraculous transformation. "So he went down and dipped himself in the Jordan seven times, as the man of God had told him, and his flesh was restored and became clean like that of a young boy" (2 Kings 5:14). The healing was complete and instantaneous, a testament to God's power and Elisha's prophetic authority.

Naaman's physical healing was accompanied by a profound spiritual awakening. The miracle led him to recognize the sovereignty of the God of Israel and to renounce his former beliefs. Returning to Elisha, Naaman stood before the prophet and declared, "Now I know that there is no God in all the world except in Israel. So please accept a gift from your servant" (2 Kings 5:15). His words reflected a significant shift in his understanding and allegiance.

Elisha, however, refused to accept any payment for the healing, emphasizing that the miracle was an act of God's grace and not something to be bought or sold. "As surely as the LORD lives, whom I serve, I will not accept a thing." And though Naaman urged him, he refused (2 Kings 5:16). Elisha's refusal reinforced the message that God's blessings are not transactional but are given freely out of His mercy and love.

Naaman's encounter with Elisha and his healing in the Jordan River taught him valuable lessons about humility, faith, and the nature of God's grace. Humbled by his experience, Naaman asked for permission to take two mule-loads of earth from Israel back to Aram, intending to build an altar to the LORD. He pledged to worship only the God of Israel from that day forward, saying, "Your servant will never again make burnt offerings and sacrifices to any other god but the LORD" (2 Kings 5:17).

Naaman's transformation extended beyond his physical healing; it marked the beginning of a new spiritual journey. He sought Elisha's understanding regarding his duties as a commander, particularly when accompanying his king into the temple of Rimmon, an Aramean deity. Naaman expressed concern about bowing in the temple, which was part of his official duties, and asked for the LORD's forgiveness in those instances.

Elisha responded with grace and understanding, saying, "Go in peace" (2 Kings 5:19). This response acknowledged Naaman's newfound faith while recognizing the complexities of his position. It highlighted the importance of a personal relationship with God and the journey of faith that Naaman had embarked upon.

## Bible Verse: 2 Kings 5:14

"So he went down and dipped himself in the Jordan seven times, as the man of God had told him, and his flesh was restored and became clean like that of a young boy."

## Reflections on Naaman's Healing

The story of Naaman's healing is rich with lessons on humility, faith, and the transformative power of God's grace. It highlights the importance of obedience to God's instructions, the significance of humility in receiving God's blessings, and the profound impact of a personal encounter with God. Several key themes emerge from this narrative, offering insights and encouragement for contemporary believers.

### The Importance of Humility

Naaman's journey to healing began with a significant challenge to his pride. As a powerful and respected commander, Naaman was accustomed to authority and reverence. Elisha's simple instructions to wash in the Jordan River seemed beneath his dignity, prompting an initial reaction of anger and rejection. However, it was only when Naaman humbled himself and followed the prophet's directive that he experienced healing.

This story teaches that humility is essential in receiving God's blessings. It requires setting aside personal pride, expectations, and preconceived notions about how God should work. Humility opens the door to God's grace and allows individuals to receive His blessings in unexpected ways. Naaman's healing underscores the truth that God's ways are higher than our ways, and His methods often challenge human pride and self-reliance.

## The Power of Faith and Obedience

Naaman's healing was a direct result of his obedience to Elisha's instructions, despite his initial doubts and objections. His decision to follow the prophet's directive, even when it seemed illogical, was an act of faith. By dipping himself in the Jordan River seven times, Naaman demonstrated his trust in the word of the man of God and, ultimately, in God's power to heal.

This aspect of the story highlights the importance of faith and obedience in experiencing God's miracles. Believers are encouraged to trust in God's instructions, even when they seem unconventional or difficult. Obedience to God's word is a demonstration of faith and a prerequisite for experiencing His transformative power. Naaman's healing challenges believers to act in faith and to trust in God's promises, even when they do not fully understand His methods.

## God's Grace and Sovereignty

The healing of Naaman is a powerful testament to God's grace and sovereignty. Despite being an outsider and a commander of a foreign army, Naaman received God's mercy and healing. His encounter with Elisha and the subsequent miracle revealed that God's grace extends beyond national and ethnic boundaries. It emphasizes that God's blessings are available to all who seek Him with a humble and contrite heart.

This story also underscores the sovereignty of God in orchestrating events and using people to accomplish His purposes. The young Israelite girl, Elisha, and Naaman's servants all played crucial roles in Naaman's journey to healing. Their faith, actions, and words were instrumental in leading Naaman to a life-changing encounter with God. The narrative highlights the interconnectedness of God's plan and the ways in which He uses various individuals to fulfill His purposes.

## The Transformative Power of a Personal Encounter with God

Naaman's healing was not just a physical transformation; it marked the beginning of a profound spiritual journey. The miracle led Naaman to recognize the sovereignty of the God of Israel and to renounce his former beliefs. His declaration of faith and his commitment to worship only the LORD reflected a deep and transformative encounter with God.

This story emphasizes the life-changing impact of a personal encounter with God. Naaman's experience challenges believers to seek a deeper relationship with God and to be open to His transformative work in their lives. It underscores the importance of personal faith and the willingness to be changed by God's grace. Naaman's journey from a proud commander to a humble servant of God serves as an example of the radical transformation that comes from encountering God's power and love.

## The Significance of Simple Acts of Faith

Elisha's instructions to Naaman were simple and unassuming: wash in the Jordan River seven times. This simplicity contrasted sharply with Naaman's expectations of a grand and elaborate ritual. However, it was through this simple act of faith that Naaman experienced healing.

This aspect of the story highlights the significance of simple acts of faith. God often works through ordinary means to accomplish extraordinary results. Believers are encouraged to embrace simplicity and to trust in God's power to work through everyday actions. Naaman's healing reminds us that profound spiritual and physical transformations can occur through simple, obedient acts of faith.

### Conclusion

The story of Naaman's healing is a powerful narrative that highlights the themes of humility, faith, and the transformative power of God's grace. Naaman's journey from a proud and powerful commander to a humble servant of God underscores the importance of humility in receiving God's blessings. His healing was a direct result of his obedience to Elisha's instructions, demonstrating the power of faith and the necessity of trusting in God's word.

This story also emphasizes God's grace and sovereignty, showing that His blessings are available to all who seek Him with a humble and contrite heart.

Naaman's transformation extended beyond his physical healing, marking the beginning of a profound spiritual journey and a personal encounter with the God of Israel.

As we reflect on this story, we are encouraged to cultivate humility, to trust in God's instructions, and to embrace simple acts of faith. Naaman's healing challenges us to seek a deeper relationship with God and to be open to His transformative work in our lives. It reminds us that God's ways are higher than our ways and that His grace and sovereignty extend beyond all boundaries.

The healing of Naaman is a testament to the enduring power of faith and the limitless potential of God's miraculous work. It invites us to trust in God's provision, to act in faith, and to experience the transformative power of a personal encounter with God. Through this story, we see the consistent nature of God's character and His ability to provide for and transform His people in miraculous ways.

# Chapter 12: Gehazi's Greed

## Gehazi's Deceit to Gain Naaman's Gifts

After the miraculous healing of Naaman, the Syrian commander, and his subsequent conversion, a new chapter unfolded in the lives of those connected to the event, particularly Gehazi, the servant of Elisha. Gehazi had witnessed the incredible power of God through his master Elisha, and he had seen Naaman's transformation from a proud, afflicted man to a humble, grateful believer in the God of Israel. However, instead of rejoicing in the miracle and the demonstration of God's power, Gehazi's heart was consumed by greed and deceit.

Naaman, overjoyed by his healing, had offered Elisha lavish gifts as a token of his gratitude. He brought ten talents of silver, six thousand shekels of gold, and ten sets of clothing, hoping to reward Elisha for the miracle. However, Elisha refused the gifts, insisting that the healing was an act of God's grace and not something that could be bought or rewarded materially. Elisha's refusal underscored the principle that God's blessings are given freely and cannot be purchased.

Despite Elisha's clear stance, Gehazi saw an opportunity to benefit personally from Naaman's generosity. As Naaman departed, Gehazi's thoughts were not on the glory of God but on the wealth that had just slipped through his fingers. Gehazi rationalized his intentions, convincing himself that taking a portion of the gifts would not harm anyone, and might even be seen as just compensation for his service.

Acting on his desire, Gehazi hurried after Naaman, catching up with him on the road. When Naaman saw Gehazi running toward him, he stopped and got down from his chariot to meet him. "Is everything all right?" Naaman asked (2 Kings 5:21). Gehazi, already caught in his web of deceit, replied with a fabricated story. "My master sent me to say, 'Two young men from the company of the prophets have just come to me from the hill country of Ephraim. Please give them a talent of silver and two sets of clothing'" (2 Kings 5:22).

Naaman, still overwhelmed with gratitude, readily agreed. "By all means, take two talents," he insisted, urging Gehazi to accept more than he had requested. Naaman even sent two of his servants to carry the silver and the clothing back with Gehazi. Gehazi's deceit was further deepened as he took the gifts, hid them in his house, and sent the servants away.

Gehazi's actions were driven by greed and a desire for personal gain. He saw an opportunity to enrich himself at the expense of honesty and integrity. His deceitful scheme was a stark contrast to the humility and righteousness exhibited by Elisha. Gehazi's actions set in motion a series of events that would have profound and tragic consequences.

## Elisha's Confrontation and the Consequence of Gehazi's Actions

Upon returning, Gehazi presented himself before Elisha, attempting to act as if nothing had happened. However, Elisha, guided by the Spirit of God, knew exactly what Gehazi had done. The prophet confronted his servant with piercing questions that revealed Gehazi's deceit. "Where have you been, Gehazi?" Elisha asked. Gehazi replied, "Your servant didn't go anywhere" (2 Kings 5:25).

Elisha's response was immediate and filled with righteous indignation. "Was not my spirit with you when the man got down from his chariot to meet you? Is this the time to take money or to accept clothes—or olive groves and vineyards, or flocks and herds, or male and female slaves?" (2 Kings 5:26). Elisha's questions cut through Gehazi's lies and exposed the greed that had driven his actions.

Elisha's confrontation highlighted the gravity of Gehazi's sin. Gehazi had not only lied and deceived, but he had also attempted to profit from a miraculous act of God's grace. His actions showed a profound disrespect for God, for Elisha's prophetic office, and for the sanctity of the miracle that had taken place. Gehazi's greed had led him to betray the principles of integrity and righteousness that Elisha upheld.

The consequences of Gehazi's actions were severe and immediate. Elisha pronounced a judgment that would change Gehazi's life forever. "Naaman's leprosy will cling to you and to your descendants forever" (2 Kings 5:27). As Elisha spoke these words, Gehazi was struck with leprosy. His skin became as white as snow, marking him as a permanent outcast and a living testament to the consequences of his greed and deceit.

# The Importance of Integrity and the Dangers of Greed

Gehazi's story serves as a powerful cautionary tale about the dangers of greed and the importance of integrity. His actions and the resulting consequences offer profound lessons for contemporary believers, emphasizing the need for honesty, humility, and a heart aligned with God's principles.

## 1. The Dangers of Greed:

Gehazi's story illustrates how greed can lead to moral compromise and spiritual downfall. His desire for material wealth blinded him to the sanctity of the miracle he had witnessed and led him to betray his master's trust. Greed distorts priorities and values, causing individuals to act in ways that are contrary to God's will. Gehazi's actions serve as a warning about the destructive power of greed and the importance of guarding one's heart against covetous desires.

## 2. The Importance of Integrity:

Elisha's integrity stood in stark contrast to Gehazi's deceit. Elisha's refusal to accept Naaman's gifts highlighted his commitment to the principle that God's blessings are not for sale. Integrity involves maintaining honesty and moral uprightness, even when faced with temptation. Gehazi's lack of integrity led to his downfall, while Elisha's steadfastness in righteousness exemplified the character that God desires in His servants.

## 3. The Consequences of Sin:

Gehazi's punishment was severe and lasting. The leprosy that afflicted him served as a tangible reminder of the consequences of his actions. Sin has consequences, and Gehazi's story underscores the reality that deceit and greed can lead to devastating outcomes. His leprosy not only marked him physically but also served as a warning to others about the seriousness of sin.

## 4. The Role of a Servant:

Gehazi's position as Elisha's servant was one of great privilege and responsibility. He was entrusted with serving the prophet and witnessing the mighty works of God. However, his actions demonstrated a failure to honor that role. Servanthood in God's kingdom requires humility, faithfulness, and a commitment to God's purposes. Gehazi's failure to embody these qualities led to his downfall.

## 5. God's Grace and Judgment:

While Gehazi's story ends with a severe judgment, it also highlights the balance between God's grace and judgment. Naaman's healing was an act of God's grace, freely given without expectation of repayment. Gehazi's punishment, though harsh, was a response to his blatant disregard for that grace and his attempt to exploit it for personal gain. The story reminds believers that God's grace is not to be taken lightly, and His judgment is a response to the misuse of His blessings.

# Bible Verse: 2 Kings 5:27

"Naaman's leprosy will cling to you and to your descendants forever." Then Gehazi went from Elisha's presence and his skin was leprous—it had become as white as snow."

# Reflections on Gehazi's Greed

Gehazi's story is a profound and sobering narrative that offers valuable lessons on the dangers of greed, the importance of integrity, and the consequences of deceit. It challenges contemporary believers to examine their own hearts and motivations, emphasizing the need for honesty, humility, and a commitment to God's principles.

## The Destructive Power of Greed

Gehazi's actions were driven by a desire for material wealth and personal gain. His greed led him to deceive Naaman, betray Elisha's trust, and ultimately suffer severe consequences. This story underscores the destructive power of greed and the ways in which it can distort priorities and values. It serves as a warning to guard against covetous desires and to prioritize spiritual integrity over material gain.

Greed is often a subtle and insidious force that can take root in the heart, leading individuals to make compromises and decisions that are contrary to God's will. Gehazi's story challenges believers to be vigilant in examining their own hearts and to root out any traces of greed. It emphasizes the importance of contentment and trust in God's provision, rather than seeking to accumulate wealth through dishonest means.

## The Importance of Integrity

Elisha's refusal to accept Naaman's gifts highlighted his commitment to integrity and righteousness. He understood that God's blessings are given freely and cannot be purchased. Gehazi's deceit, in contrast, demonstrated a lack of integrity and a willingness to compromise moral principles for personal gain.

Integrity involves maintaining honesty and moral uprightness, even when faced with temptation. It requires a commitment to doing what is right, regardless of the potential for personal benefit. Gehazi's story underscores the importance of integrity in the life of a believer and the need to uphold God's standards in all aspects of life. It challenges believers to be people of integrity, who are faithful to God's principles and who resist the temptation to compromise for personal gain.

## The Consequences of Sin

The severe consequences of Gehazi's actions serve as a stark reminder of the reality of sin and its impact. Gehazi's leprosy was a tangible and lasting punishment that marked him as an outcast and a warning to others. This story highlights the seriousness of sin and the importance of recognizing its consequences.

Sin has real and lasting consequences, both in this life and in the life to come. Gehazi's punishment serves as a reminder that deceit, greed, and moral compromise can lead to devastating outcomes. It challenges believers to take sin seriously and to strive for righteousness in all aspects of their lives. It also underscores the importance of seeking God's forgiveness and grace when we fall short, recognizing that His mercy is available to those who repent.

## The Role of Servanthood

Gehazi's position as Elisha's servant was one of great privilege and responsibility. He was entrusted with serving the prophet and witnessing the mighty works of God. However, his actions demonstrated a failure to honor that role. Servanthood in God's kingdom requires humility, faithfulness, and a commitment to God's purposes.

Gehazi's story challenges believers to embrace the role of servanthood with humility and faithfulness. It emphasizes the importance of serving others with integrity and a heart aligned with God's will. Believers are called to be faithful stewards of the responsibilities and opportunities God has given them, recognizing that true greatness in God's kingdom is found in humble service.

## God's Grace and Judgment

While Gehazi's story ends with a severe judgment, it also highlights the balance between God's grace and judgment. Naaman's healing was an act of God's grace, freely given without expectation of repayment. Gehazi's punishment, though harsh, was a response to his blatant disregard for that grace and his attempt to exploit it for personal gain.

This story reminds believers that God's grace is a precious gift that should not be taken lightly. It emphasizes the importance of responding to God's grace with gratitude and humility, rather than seeking to exploit it for personal gain. Gehazi's story also underscores the reality of God's judgment and the need to live in a way that honors His grace and upholds His principles.

### Conclusion

The story of Gehazi's greed is a powerful and sobering narrative that highlights the dangers of greed, the importance of integrity, and the consequences of deceit. Gehazi's actions and the resulting punishment serve as a cautionary tale for contemporary believers, emphasizing the need for honesty, humility, and a heart aligned with God's principles.

As we reflect on this story, we are challenged to examine our own hearts and motivations. Gehazi's story underscores the destructive power of greed and the ways in which it can lead to moral compromise and spiritual downfall. It challenges us to guard against covetous desires and to prioritize spiritual integrity over material gain.

The importance of integrity is a central lesson from this story. Elisha's refusal to accept Naaman's gifts and his commitment to righteousness serve as a powerful example of the character that God desires in His servants. Gehazi's lack of integrity and willingness to deceive highlight the need for honesty and moral uprightness in all aspects of life.

The severe consequences of Gehazi's actions remind us of the reality of sin and its impact. Gehazi's leprosy was a tangible and lasting punishment that underscored the seriousness of his actions. This story challenges us to take sin seriously and to strive for righteousness, recognizing the importance of seeking God's forgiveness and grace when we fall short.

The role of servanthood is another key theme in this story. Gehazi's position as Elisha's servant was one of great privilege and responsibility, yet he failed to honor that role. This story challenges us to embrace the role of servanthood with humility and faithfulness, recognizing that true greatness in God's kingdom is found in humble service.

Finally, Gehazi's story highlights the balance between God's grace and judgment. Naaman's healing was an act of God's grace, freely given, while Gehazi's punishment was a response to his blatant disregard for that grace. This story reminds us of the preciousness of God's grace and the importance of responding to it with gratitude and humility.

The story of Gehazi's greed is a powerful testament to the enduring importance of integrity, the dangers of greed, and the transformative power of God's grace. It invites us to live lives marked by honesty, humility, and a deep commitment to God's principles, recognizing that true fulfillment and blessing come from aligning our hearts with His will. Through this story, we see the consistent nature of God's character and His desire for His people to walk in righteousness and integrity.

# Chapter 13: The Floating Axe Head

## The Loss of a Borrowed Axe Head by One of the Prophets

In the time of Elisha, the community of prophets, also known as the sons of the prophets, lived and worked together, often under the direct guidance of Elisha. These young men were dedicated to studying the ways of God and serving Him, learning from Elisha's example and instruction. Their communal life was one of simplicity, mutual support, and a shared commitment to their divine calling.

As their numbers grew, they found that their living quarters had become too small to accommodate everyone comfortably. In response, they decided to expand their living space by building a larger meeting place near the Jordan River. This project required significant manual labor, including cutting down trees to obtain the necessary timber for construction.

One day, as the prophets were busy felling trees near the Jordan River, a mishap occurred. One of the young prophets was using an axe to cut down a tree when the iron axe head flew off the handle and fell into the river. The young man was immediately distressed, not only because the axe was essential for their work, but also because it was borrowed. In ancient Israel, borrowing tools and equipment was common practice, and losing or damaging borrowed items carried serious implications. The prophet's distress was evident as he exclaimed to Elisha, "Oh no, my lord! It was borrowed!" (2 Kings 6:5).

The loss of the axe head was a significant problem for the young prophet. Iron tools were valuable and relatively scarce, making their replacement costly and difficult. Furthermore, the borrowed nature of the axe meant that the young man was now indebted to the owner, adding to his anxiety. The situation seemed dire, as the heavy iron axe head had sunk to the bottom of the river, making its recovery appear impossible.

# Elisha's Miraculous Recovery of the Axe Head from the Water

Elisha, upon hearing the young prophet's distressed cry, responded with compassion and practicality. He asked the young man to show him the exact spot where the axe head had fallen. "The man of God asked, 'Where did it fall?' When he showed him the place, Elisha cut a stick and threw it there, and made the iron float" (2 Kings 6:6).

Elisha's actions were both simple and profound. By asking the young prophet to point out the location, Elisha demonstrated his attentiveness and willingness to address the seemingly minor concern. Cutting a stick and throwing it into the water was a symbolic act, reminiscent of other prophetic gestures seen throughout the Bible. This act of faith and obedience served as a conduit for God's miraculous intervention.

To the amazement of the prophets, the iron axe head floated to the surface of the water, defying the laws of nature. Elisha instructed the young man to retrieve it, saying, "Lift it out." The young prophet reached out his hand and took the axe head, his relief and gratitude evident (2 Kings 6:7). This miraculous recovery not only resolved the immediate problem but also reinforced the faith of the prophets in God's provision and care.

# God's Care for the Small Needs of His People

The miracle of the floating axe head is a powerful testament to God's care for the small and seemingly insignificant needs of His people. While the event might appear minor compared to other grand miracles in the Bible, it holds profound lessons about God's attentiveness, compassion, and willingness to intervene in the everyday lives of His followers.

## 1. God's Attentiveness to Our Needs:

The story of the floating axe head highlights God's attentiveness to the needs of His people, no matter how small or insignificant they may seem. The young prophet's distress over the loss of the borrowed axe head was met with a miraculous response, demonstrating that God is concerned with every aspect of our lives. This lesson encourages believers to bring all their concerns to God, trusting that He cares deeply about their well-being.

## 2. The Importance of Faith and Obedience:

Elisha's actions in retrieving the axe head involved a simple act of faith and obedience. By cutting a stick and throwing it into the water, Elisha demonstrated his trust in God's power to perform miracles. This story underscores the importance of faith and obedience in experiencing God's intervention. Believers are encouraged to act in faith, even when the solution to their problems seems impossible.

## 3. God's Provision in Everyday Life:

The miraculous recovery of the axe head serves as a reminder that God's provision extends to the practical and mundane aspects of life. While grand miracles often capture our attention, God's care is equally evident in the small, everyday blessings. This story challenges believers to recognize and appreciate God's provision in all areas of their lives, trusting that He is present and active in both the extraordinary and the ordinary.

## 4. The Value of Community and Mutual Support:

The communal life of the prophets, their shared efforts in building a larger meeting place, and their collective witness of the miracle highlight the importance of community and mutual support. The young prophet's distress was met with immediate concern and action from Elisha and the rest of the group. This story emphasizes the value of living in a supportive community where individuals care for one another and work together to address challenges.

## 5. The Role of Prophetic Leadership:

Elisha's role as a prophet and leader was crucial in guiding and supporting the young prophets. His willingness to address the young man's concern and his ability to facilitate a miraculous solution demonstrated his dedication to serving and nurturing the community. This story underscores the importance of prophetic leadership in providing spiritual guidance and practical support to God's people.

# Bible Verse: 2 Kings 6:6

"The man of God asked, 'Where did it fall?' When he showed him the place, Elisha cut a stick and threw it there, and made the iron float."

# Reflections on the Floating Axe Head

The story of the floating axe head is rich with spiritual insights and lessons that are relevant for contemporary believers. It highlights God's attentiveness to our needs, the importance of faith and obedience, the value of community, and the role of prophetic leadership. Several key themes emerge from this narrative, offering encouragement and guidance for our daily lives.

## God's Attentiveness to Our Needs

One of the central themes of this story is God's attentiveness to the needs of His people. The young prophet's distress over the loss of the borrowed axe head might seem trivial in the grand scheme of things, yet it mattered to God. Elisha's immediate response and the miraculous recovery of the axe head demonstrate that God is concerned with every aspect of our lives, no matter how small or insignificant it may seem.

This lesson is a source of comfort and encouragement for believers. It reassures them that God is aware of their struggles and concerns, and He is willing to intervene and provide solutions. The story challenges believers to bring all their needs and concerns to God, trusting that He cares deeply about their well-being. It emphasizes the importance of maintaining a relationship with God where we feel comfortable sharing every aspect of our lives with Him.

## The Importance of Faith and Obedience

Elisha's actions in retrieving the axe head involved a simple act of faith and obedience. By cutting a stick and throwing it into the water, Elisha demonstrated his trust in God's power to perform miracles. This story underscores the importance of faith and obedience in experiencing God's intervention. Believers are encouraged to act in faith, even when the solution to their problems seems impossible.

Faith and obedience are essential components of the Christian walk. The story of the floating axe head challenges believers to trust in God's instructions and to act in faith, even when they do not fully understand how God will work. It encourages believers to step out in faith and to be obedient to God's leading, trusting that He will provide and perform miracles in their lives.

## God's Provision in Everyday Life

The miraculous recovery of the axe head serves as a reminder that God's provision extends to the practical and mundane aspects of life. While grand miracles often capture our attention, God's care is equally evident in the small, everyday blessings. This story challenges believers to recognize and appreciate God's provision in all areas of their lives, trusting that He is present and active in both the extraordinary and the ordinary.

Believers are encouraged to cultivate an attitude of gratitude, recognizing and appreciating God's provision in their daily lives. The story of the floating axe head invites believers to see God's hand in the small and seemingly insignificant details of their lives and to trust that He is attentive to their needs.

## The Value of Community and Mutual Support

The communal life of the prophets, their shared efforts in building a larger meeting place, and their collective witness of the miracle highlight the importance of community and mutual support. The young prophet's distress was met with immediate concern and action from Elisha and the rest of the group. This story emphasizes the value of living in a supportive community where individuals care for one another and work together to address challenges.

Community and mutual support are vital aspects of the Christian faith. Believers are called to live in community, supporting and encouraging one another in their walk with God. The story of the floating axe head underscores the importance of being part of a community where individuals are attentive to each other's needs and willing to offer help and support. It challenges believers to foster a sense of community and to be proactive in supporting and caring for one another.

## The Role of Prophetic Leadership

Elisha's role as a prophet and leader was crucial in guiding and supporting the young prophets. His willingness to address the young man's concern and his ability to facilitate a miraculous solution demonstrated his dedication to serving and nurturing the community. This story underscores the importance of prophetic leadership in providing spiritual guidance and practical support to God's people.

Prophetic leadership involves guiding, nurturing, and supporting God's people in their spiritual journey. Elisha's actions serve as a model for contemporary spiritual leaders, emphasizing the importance of being attentive to the needs of those they lead and being willing to seek God's intervention on their behalf. The story challenges spiritual leaders to be compassionate, proactive, and faithful in their service to God's people.

### Conclusion

The story of the floating axe head is a powerful narrative that highlights God's attentiveness to our needs, the importance of faith and obedience, the value of community, and the role of prophetic leadership. It serves as a testament to God's care for the small and seemingly insignificant aspects of our lives and challenges believers to trust in His provision and intervention.

As we reflect on this story, we are encouraged to bring all our concerns to God, trusting that He cares deeply about every aspect of our lives. The story underscores the importance of faith and obedience, challenging us to act in faith and to trust in God's instructions, even when the solution seems impossible.

The miraculous recovery of the axe head reminds us of God's provision in everyday life and challenges us to recognize and appreciate His hand in the small details of our lives. It encourages us to cultivate an attitude of gratitude and to trust that God is attentive to our needs.

The communal life of the prophets and their mutual support highlight the importance of living in a supportive community where individuals care for one another. The story challenges us to foster a sense of community and to be proactive in supporting and caring for one another.

Finally, Elisha's role as a prophetic leader underscores the importance of spiritual leadership in guiding and nurturing God's people. The story challenges spiritual leaders to be attentive, compassionate, and proactive in their service, seeking God's intervention on behalf of those they lead.

The story of the floating axe head is a powerful testament to God's care, provision, and intervention in our lives. It invites us to trust in God's attentiveness to our needs, to act in faith and obedience, to appreciate His provision in everyday life, to foster a sense of community, and to recognize the vital role of prophetic leadership. Through this story, we see the consistent nature of God's character and His desire to be involved in every aspect of our lives, providing for and caring for His people in miraculous ways.

# Chapter 14: The Blinded Arameans

## The Aramean Army Surrounds Elisha

During the time of Elisha, Israel faced continual threats from neighboring nations, one of the most persistent being the kingdom of Aram. The Arameans, under the leadership of their king, frequently raided and attacked Israel, seeking to weaken and destabilize the nation. Amidst this backdrop of conflict, Elisha's prophetic ministry played a crucial role in guiding and protecting the people of Israel.

Elisha, a prophet of great renown, had become a significant thorn in the side of the Aramean king. Through divine revelation, Elisha was able to thwart the Aramean military strategies, warning the king of Israel about their movements and plans. Time and again, Elisha's prophetic insight saved Israel from potential disaster, frustrating the Aramean king's efforts and leading him to suspect a traitor within his ranks.

Upon learning that it was Elisha, the prophet in Israel, who was revealing his plans, the Aramean king decided to eliminate the source of his troubles. He dispatched a substantial military force to Dothan, where Elisha was staying. Under the cover of night, the Aramean army surrounded the city, intending to capture or kill the prophet. The sight of the formidable enemy force encircling the city was enough to strike fear into the hearts of its inhabitants.

Early the next morning, Elisha's servant awoke and went outside, only to be met with the alarming sight of the Aramean army. Panicked and overwhelmed by fear, he rushed back to Elisha, exclaiming, "Oh no, my lord! What shall we do?" (2 Kings 6:15). The young servant's terror was palpable, reflecting the apparent hopelessness of their situation.

Elisha, however, remained calm and composed, his faith in God unshaken. He reassured his servant with words that revealed a deeper, spiritual reality beyond what was visible to the human eye. "Don't be afraid," the prophet answered. "Those who are with us are more than those who are with them" (2 Kings 6:16). To the frightened servant, Elisha's words must have seemed incredulous, given the overwhelming military presence outside.

Elisha then prayed, asking God to open his servant's eyes to see the divine protection surrounding them. "Open his eyes, LORD, so that he may see" (2 Kings 6:17). In response to Elisha's prayer, God opened the servant's eyes, allowing him to see the spiritual realm. The servant saw the hills full of horses and chariots of fire all around Elisha, a heavenly army sent by God to protect His prophet. This divine revelation transformed the servant's fear into awe and confidence, knowing that God's mighty forces were on their side.

## Elisha's Prayer to Blind the Enemy Soldiers

With the Aramean army closing in, Elisha demonstrated not only his unwavering faith but also his reliance on divine intervention. As the enemy forces advanced, Elisha prayed to the LORD to strike them with blindness. "Strike this army with blindness," Elisha prayed, and God responded to his request. "So he struck them with blindness, as Elisha had asked" (2 Kings 6:18).

The sudden onset of blindness among the Aramean soldiers was a miraculous act of God, turning their formidable strength into vulnerability. The soldiers, now disoriented and unable to see, were rendered helpless. This divine intervention showcased God's power to protect His people and confound their enemies. Elisha's prayer and the subsequent miracle highlighted the prophet's close relationship with God and his ability to call upon divine aid in times of crisis.

Elisha then approached the blind and confused soldiers, taking advantage of their condition to lead them away from Dothan. He told them, "This is not the road and this is not the city. Follow me, and I will lead you to the man you are looking for." Deceived by their blindness, the soldiers followed Elisha, unaware that he was leading them into the heart of Samaria, the capital of Israel (2 Kings 6:19).

The journey to Samaria must have been one of confusion and uncertainty for the Aramean soldiers, unable to see and reliant on Elisha's guidance. Upon reaching Samaria, Elisha prayed once more, asking God to open their eyes. "LORD, open the eyes of these men so they can see." God answered Elisha's prayer, and the soldiers' sight was restored. To their shock and dismay, they found themselves surrounded by the Israelite army within the fortified city of Samaria (2 Kings 6:20).

# The Capture and Merciful Release of the Aramean Soldiers

The Aramean soldiers, now fully aware of their precarious situation, were at the mercy of the Israelites. The king of Israel, seeing the enemy forces within his grasp, asked Elisha, "Shall I kill them, my father? Shall I kill them?" (2 Kings 6:21). The king's eagerness to eliminate the threat was understandable, given the persistent hostilities between Israel and Aram.

However, Elisha's response was unexpected and merciful. "Do not kill them," he answered. "Would you kill those you have captured with your own sword or bow? Set food and water before them so that they may eat and drink and then go back to their master" (2 Kings 6:22). Elisha's directive was a call to show mercy and hospitality, even to their enemies.

The king of Israel followed Elisha's instructions, preparing a great feast for the captured soldiers. After they had eaten and drunk, he sent them back to their master. This act of mercy and kindness had a profound impact on the Aramean soldiers and their king. Rather than responding with hostility, the king of Aram ceased his raids into Israel's territory for a time, fostering a period of peace between the two nations (2 Kings 6:23).

Elisha's handling of the situation demonstrated the power of mercy and the potential for reconciliation, even in the midst of conflict. His actions illustrated the principle that showing kindness to one's enemies can lead to unexpected and positive outcomes. The story of the blinded Arameans and their merciful release serves as a powerful reminder of the transformative power of mercy and the ways in which God can work through acts of compassion.

## Bible Verse: 2 Kings 6:18

"As the enemy came down toward him, Elisha prayed to the LORD, 'Strike this army with blindness.' So he struck them with blindness, as Elisha had asked."

# Reflections on the Blinded Arameans

The story of the blinded Arameans is rich with lessons on faith, divine intervention, mercy, and the transformative power of God's actions. It highlights the importance of trusting in God's protection, the power of prayer, and the impact of showing mercy to one's enemies. Several key themes emerge from this narrative, offering insights and encouragement for contemporary believers.

## Faith in God's Protection

Elisha's calm demeanor in the face of the Aramean threat exemplifies unwavering faith in God's protection. Despite being surrounded by a formidable enemy force, Elisha's trust in God did not waver. His assurance to his servant, "Those who are with us are more than those who are with them" (2 Kings 6:16), reflects a deep awareness of God's presence and power.

This story encourages believers to have faith in God's protection, even when circumstances seem dire. It reassures them that God is always with them, and His divine protection is far greater than any earthly threat. The vision of the heavenly army surrounding Elisha serves as a powerful reminder that God's forces are always at work, safeguarding His people.

## The Power of Prayer

Elisha's prayers played a central role in the events of this story. His prayer for his servant's eyes to be opened and his prayer to strike the Aramean soldiers with blindness were both answered by God, demonstrating the power of prayer to bring about divine intervention. Elisha's reliance on prayer highlights the importance of seeking God's help and guidance in times of need.

This story underscores the significance of prayer in the life of a believer. It encourages believers to pray with faith and confidence, trusting that God hears and responds to their prayers. Elisha's example challenges believers to cultivate a strong prayer life, recognizing that prayer is a powerful tool for accessing God's assistance and intervention.

## Divine Intervention in Times of Crisis

The miraculous blinding of the Aramean soldiers is a testament to God's ability to intervene in times of crisis. By striking the soldiers with blindness, God turned a seemingly hopeless situation into an opportunity for His power and mercy to be displayed. This divine intervention protected Elisha and the inhabitants of Dothan, demonstrating God's sovereignty over all circumstances.

Believers are encouraged to trust in God's ability to intervene in their lives, especially during times of crisis. The story of the blinded Arameans reminds them that God is always in control and capable of performing miracles to protect and deliver His people. It challenges believers to maintain faith and hope, even in the face of overwhelming challenges.

## The Transformative Power of Mercy

Elisha's decision to show mercy to the captured Aramean soldiers was a profound demonstration of compassion and forgiveness. Instead of advocating for their destruction, Elisha instructed the king of Israel to provide them with food and water and then release them. This act of mercy had a significant impact, leading to a temporary cessation of hostilities between Israel and Aram.

This story highlights the transformative power of mercy and the potential for reconciliation through acts of kindness. It challenges believers to show mercy and compassion to their enemies, recognizing that such actions can lead to positive and unexpected outcomes. Elisha's example encourages believers to respond to conflict with grace and to seek opportunities for reconciliation and peace.

## God's Sovereignty and Wisdom

The story of the blinded Arameans underscores God's sovereignty and wisdom in orchestrating events. God's intervention through Elisha's prayers and the subsequent actions taken demonstrate His control over all situations. The miraculous blinding and the merciful release of the soldiers were all part of God's plan to protect His people and promote peace.

Believers are reminded of God's sovereignty and wisdom in their own lives. The story encourages them to trust in God's plan and to seek His guidance in all circumstances. It reassures them that God's ways are higher than their ways, and His wisdom is beyond human understanding. By trusting in God's sovereignty, believers can find peace and confidence in the midst of challenges.

## Conclusion

The story of the blinded Arameans is a powerful narrative that highlights the themes of faith, divine intervention, mercy, and the transformative power of God's actions. Elisha's calm faith in God's protection, the power of his prayers, and his decision to show mercy to the captured soldiers all offer valuable lessons for contemporary believers.

As we reflect on this story, we are encouraged to have faith in God's protection, trusting that He is always with us and capable of safeguarding us from harm. The vision of the heavenly army surrounding Elisha serves as a powerful reminder of God's presence and power.

The power of prayer is another key lesson from this story. Elisha's reliance on prayer underscores the importance of seeking God's help and guidance in times of need. This story challenges believers to cultivate a strong prayer life and to pray with faith and confidence, trusting that God hears and responds to their prayers.

The miraculous blinding of the Aramean soldiers demonstrates God's ability to intervene in times of crisis. This story encourages believers to trust in God's sovereignty and to maintain faith and hope, even in the face of overwhelming challenges.

Elisha's decision to show mercy to the captured soldiers highlights the transformative power of compassion and forgiveness. This story challenges believers to respond to conflict with grace and to seek opportunities for reconciliation and peace. Elisha's example encourages us to show mercy and kindness to our enemies, recognizing that such actions can lead to positive and unexpected outcomes.

Finally, the story of the blinded Arameans underscores God's sovereignty and wisdom in orchestrating events. It reminds us to trust in God's plan and to seek His guidance in all circumstances. By trusting in God's sovereignty, we can find peace and confidence in the midst of challenges.

The story of the blinded Arameans is a powerful testament to God's care, protection, and intervention in our lives. It invites us to trust in His presence, to pray with faith, to show mercy and compassion, and to rely on His sovereignty and wisdom. Through this story, we see the consistent nature of God's character and His desire to work through acts of faith, prayer, and mercy to bring about His purposes and promote peace.

# Chapter 15: The Siege of Samaria

## The Famine and Desperation in Samaria Due to the Aramean Siege

The city of Samaria, the capital of the northern kingdom of Israel, was under siege by the Aramean army. This prolonged siege had led to a severe famine within the city walls, pushing the inhabitants to the brink of despair. The Aramean forces had cut off all supplies, and the resulting scarcity of food had driven the prices of basic necessities to unimaginable heights. The people of Samaria were facing extreme hunger, and the situation grew more dire with each passing day.

The famine in Samaria was not just a crisis of hunger but a profound test of the people's faith and endurance. As the siege dragged on, the desperation within the city reached its peak. The biblical account details horrifying acts born out of extreme hunger, including instances of cannibalism. The king of Israel, upon witnessing such atrocities, was stricken with grief and anger. In his desperation, he blamed Elisha, the prophet of God, for the city's suffering and swore to have him executed.

Elisha remained calm and steadfast despite the king's threats. He understood that the famine and siege were part of a larger divine plan, and he awaited God's intervention with unwavering faith. The king's messenger, sent to capture Elisha, found him sitting with the elders of Israel. Elisha's prophetic insight allowed him to foresee the king's intention, and he spoke with authority, predicting the imminent deliverance of Samaria.

## Elisha's Prophecy of Abundant Food

Amid the chaos and desperation, Elisha delivered a bold prophecy that seemed impossible given the current circumstances. "Hear the word of the LORD. This is what the LORD says: About this time tomorrow, a seah of the finest flour will sell for a shekel and two seahs of barley for a shekel at the gate of Samaria" (2 Kings 7:1). Elisha's declaration promised an abundance of food at remarkably low prices within twenty-four hours, a statement that must have sounded utterly preposterous to those suffering from the famine.

One of the king's officers, skeptical of Elisha's prophecy, voiced his doubt. "Look, even if the LORD should open the floodgates of the heavens, could this happen?" (2 Kings 7:2). Elisha responded with a sobering message: "You will see it with your own eyes," he answered, "but you will not eat any of it!" (2 Kings 7:2). This exchange highlighted the tension between faith in God's word and the skepticism born out of dire circumstances.

Elisha's prophecy was not just a promise of physical deliverance but a test of faith for the people of Samaria. It challenged them to believe in the power of God to transform their situation radically and instantaneously. The prophecy set the stage for a miraculous intervention that would demonstrate God's sovereignty and provision in the face of human impossibility.

## The Miraculous Deliverance of Samaria and the Fulfillment of Elisha's Prophecy

As night fell over the besieged city, four men suffering from leprosy, who were considered outcasts and forced to live outside the city gates, deliberated their grim fate. They reasoned among themselves that remaining where they were meant certain death, either from the famine within the city or from their condition outside. In a desperate bid for survival, they decided to go to the Aramean camp, reasoning that surrender might at least grant them a chance at mercy and food.

When the lepers reached the Aramean camp at twilight, they were astonished to find it deserted. Unknown to them, the Lord had caused the Arameans to hear the sound of a great army approaching, including chariots and horses, leading them to believe that the Israelites had hired Hittite and Egyptian forces to attack them. In a panic, the Arameans fled, abandoning their tents, horses, donkeys, and provisions, and leaving everything behind as they fled for their lives (2 Kings 7:6-7).

The lepers entered one of the tents, ate and drank their fill, and took silver, gold, and clothing. Realizing the enormity of what they had discovered, they said to each other, "What we're doing is not right. This is a day of good news and we are keeping it to ourselves. If we wait until daylight, punishment will overtake us. Let's go at once and report this to the royal palace" (2 Kings 7:9). Driven by a sense of responsibility, they returned to the city and reported their findings to the gatekeepers, who relayed the news to the king's palace.

Initially skeptical, the king suspected a trap, believing the Arameans had left their camp to lure the Israelites out of the city. To verify the lepers' report, he sent scouts with instructions to follow the trail of the fleeing Arameans. The scouts confirmed the lepers' account, finding the road strewn with clothing and equipment discarded by the panicked soldiers. Upon receiving this confirmation, the people of Samaria rushed out and plundered the abandoned Aramean camp, finding an abundance of food and supplies.

As Elisha had prophesied, the sudden influx of provisions caused the prices of food to plummet. A seah of the finest flour sold for a shekel, and two seahs of barley for a shekel, just as Elisha had foretold. The miraculous deliverance of Samaria was a powerful demonstration of God's sovereignty and His ability to provide for His people in the most desperate circumstances.

The skeptical officer, who had doubted Elisha's prophecy, was assigned to manage the gate as the people rushed out to plunder the Aramean camp. In the ensuing chaos, he was trampled to death by the crowd, fulfilling Elisha's grim prediction that he would see the miraculous provision but not partake of it (2 Kings 7:17-20). This tragic end underscored the consequences of unbelief and skepticism in the face of God's promises.

## Bible Verse: 2 Kings 7:1

"Elisha replied, 'Hear the word of the LORD. This is what the LORD says: About this time tomorrow, a seah of the finest flour will sell for a shekel and two seahs of barley for a shekel at the gate of Samaria.'"

## Reflections on the Siege of Samaria

The story of the siege of Samaria is rich with lessons on faith, divine provision, and the power of prophecy. It highlights the importance of trusting in God's promises, even in the face of overwhelming circumstances, and the consequences of doubt and skepticism. Several key themes emerge from this narrative, offering insights and encouragement for contemporary believers.

# The Power of Divine Provision

The miraculous deliverance of Samaria underscores the power of God's provision in the most desperate circumstances. The famine and siege had brought the city to the brink of despair, yet God's intervention transformed a situation of scarcity into one of abundance. The sudden availability of food at affordable prices was a powerful demonstration of God's ability to provide for His people beyond human understanding.

This story encourages believers to trust in God's provision, even when faced with seemingly insurmountable challenges. It reassures them that God is aware of their needs and capable of providing for them in ways that surpass their expectations. The narrative challenges believers to maintain faith in God's promises and to trust that He can transform their circumstances in miraculous ways.

# The Importance of Faith in God's Promises

Elisha's prophecy of abundant food was a bold declaration of faith in God's promises. Despite the dire circumstances, Elisha confidently proclaimed that God would provide for the city within twenty-four hours. His faith in God's word stood in stark contrast to the skepticism of the king's officer, who doubted the possibility of such a miraculous turnaround.

This story highlights the importance of faith in God's promises. Believers are encouraged to trust in God's word and to hold on to His promises, even when circumstances seem hopeless. Elisha's example challenges believers to have unwavering faith in God's ability to fulfill His promises and to expect His intervention in their lives.

# The Consequences of Skepticism and Unbelief

The tragic end of the skeptical officer serves as a sobering reminder of the consequences of unbelief. His doubt in Elisha's prophecy prevented him from partaking in the miraculous provision and led to his death. This aspect of the story underscores the dangers of skepticism and the importance of responding to God's promises with faith.

Believers are challenged to examine their own hearts for doubt and unbelief and to cultivate a spirit of faith and trust in God's promises. The story of the siege of Samaria encourages believers to overcome skepticism and to embrace God's word with confidence and expectation.

## The Role of Prophetic Leadership

Elisha's role as a prophet and leader was crucial in guiding the people of Samaria through their crisis. His bold prophecy, unwavering faith, and reliance on God's guidance provided hope and direction in the midst of despair. Elisha's actions demonstrated the importance of prophetic leadership in times of crisis.

This story underscores the value of prophetic leadership in providing spiritual guidance and encouragement to God's people. Believers are encouraged to seek and support prophetic leaders who can help them navigate challenging circumstances with faith and wisdom. Elisha's example challenges spiritual leaders to speak boldly, trust in God's promises, and guide their communities with confidence in God's provision.

## The Transformative Power of God's Intervention

The miraculous deliverance of Samaria is a testament to the transformative power of God's intervention. The city's desperate situation was radically changed by a single act of divine provision, turning famine into abundance and despair into hope. This story highlights the potential for God's intervention to bring about profound and positive change.

Believers are reminded of God's ability to transform their circumstances through His intervention. The story encourages them to maintain hope and faith, trusting that God can bring about significant change in their lives. It challenges believers to be open to God's transformative power and to expect His intervention in ways that defy human understanding.

### Conclusion

The story of the siege of Samaria is a powerful narrative that highlights the themes of faith, divine provision, and the power of prophecy. Elisha's bold prophecy, the miraculous deliverance of the city, and the consequences of skepticism offer valuable lessons for contemporary believers.

As we reflect on this story, we are encouraged to trust in God's provision, even in the face of overwhelming challenges. The miraculous deliverance of Samaria reassures us that God is aware of our needs and capable of providing for us in ways that surpass our expectations. It challenges us to maintain faith in God's promises and to trust that He can transform our circumstances in miraculous ways.

The importance of faith in God's promises is another key lesson from this story. Elisha's bold declaration of God's provision challenges us to trust in God's word and to hold on to His promises, even when circumstances seem hopeless. The story encourages us to overcome skepticism and to embrace God's word with confidence and expectation.

The tragic end of the skeptical officer serves as a sobering reminder of the consequences of unbelief. It challenges us to examine our own hearts for doubt and unbelief and to cultivate a spirit of faith and trust in God's promises.

Elisha's role as a prophetic leader underscores the importance of spiritual guidance in times of crisis. The story encourages us to seek and support prophetic leaders who can help us navigate challenging circumstances with faith and wisdom. It challenges spiritual leaders to speak boldly, trust in God's promises, and guide their communities with confidence in God's provision.

Finally, the miraculous deliverance of Samaria highlights the transformative power of God's intervention. The story reminds us of God's ability to transform our circumstances through His intervention and encourages us to maintain hope and faith. It challenges us to be open to God's transformative power and to expect His intervention in ways that defy human understanding.

The story of the siege of Samaria is a powerful testament to God's care, provision, and intervention in our lives. It invites us to trust in His presence, to embrace His promises with faith, and to rely on His transformative power. Through this story, we see the consistent nature of God's character and His desire to work through acts of faith and prophecy to bring about His purposes and provide for His people.

# Don't miss out!

Visit the website below and you can sign up to receive emails whenever Gregory Allen Parker publishes a new book. There's no charge and no obligation.

https://books2read.com/r/B-A-SLYZB-OGHGE

**BOOKS 2 READ**

Connecting independent readers to independent writers.

Did you love *The Miracles of Elisha*? Then you should read *In His Footsteps*[1] by Gregory Allen Parker!

"In His Footsteps: A Collection of Christian Fiction" offers fifteen inspiring stories, each centered around a biblical parable or teaching. From the journey of the prodigal son to the hope of resurrection, these narratives illustrate profound spiritual truths and the transformative power of faith. Each chapter concludes with reflections and prayers, encouraging readers to apply these lessons to their own lives. Whether it's through acts of kindness, personal growth, or trusting God's guidance, this collection showcases the timeless message of God's love and grace.

---

1. https://books2read.com/u/brQ17e

2. https://books2read.com/u/brQ17e

# About the Author

Pastor Gregory Allen Parker, a graduate of Trinity Theological Seminary, is a devoted pastor and acclaimed author of Christian fiction. With over two decades of ministry experience, his books explore faith's challenges and triumphs, offering readers inspiring and spiritually rich narratives. Celebrated for his compassionate pastoral care and insightful sermons, Pastor Parker's storytelling reflects his deep understanding of Christian values. When not writing or preaching, he enjoys family time, community volunteering, and the outdoors, continuing to inspire and uplift through his faith and craft.

www.ingramcontent.com/pod-product-compliance
Lightning Source LLC
Chambersburg PA
CBHW031432150726
47989CB00002B/918